Some of the Things I Did Not Do

A list of books in the series appears at the end of this volume.

Some of the Things I Did Not Do

Stories by
Janet Beeler Shaw

UNIVERSITY OF ILLINOIS PRESS

Urbana and Chicago

*Publication of this work was supported in part
by grants from the National Endowment for the Arts
and the Illinois Arts Council, a state agency.*

This book is printed on acid-free paper.

"A New Life," *The Atlantic Monthly* 252, no. 4 (October 1983)
"Love and Other Lessons," *The Atlantic Monthly* 250, no. 2 (August 1982)
"In High Country," *Southwest Review* 67, no. 3 (Summer 1982)
"Saturday Night in Pinedale, Wyoming," *Triquarterly 51* (Spring 1981)
"The Trail to the Ledge," *Southwest Review* 65, no. 2 (Spring 1980)

Library of Congress Cataloging in Publication Data

Shaw, Janet Beeler, 1937–
  Some of the things I did not do.

  (Illinois short fiction)
  I. Title. II. Series.
PS3552.E345S6   1984   813'.54   83-18319
ISBN 0-252-01109-0

For Bob,
and for Kristin, Mark, and Laura Beeler

Contents

Love and Other Lessons

Of the four pay phones in Highwood that Lina Jean could use, the one she liked the least was the booth in front of the truck stop on Route 285. Even when she closed the glass doors tight, the mountain wind and the heave of passing trucks shook the walls and drowned out whole sentences. Once a Coors truck driver veered close as if he might hit the booth. He grinned down at her when she flinched. Then he puckered her a kiss and winked; he must have guessed that she was calling a man. Anyone who saw the way she pressed the receiver to her ear, pushed her forehead against the chrome, and hunched her shoulders against the invasion of traffic noises could have guessed that.

There wasn't much more privacy at the wall phone in the vestibule of the Mountain Inn Café, but here Lina Jean didn't have to worry about the trucks. "No rooms in the Inn!" Alberta Pollack, who ran the café, liked to say as she made change. "Nothing here but the best fried chicken in Colorado!" Lina Jean wasn't bothered by the people who passed her, but Alberta stared and stared, even when she was ringing up a check and repeating her dried-up old joke. So of course Alberta knew, too. How could Lina Jean mask the flush of disappointment at the base of her throat when he wasn't there to answer her call? She had no disguises. And if Alberta knew, the whole town must know.

The pay phone in the New Day Coin Laundry was better. The New Day was really just a basement with a few washers and dryers. The phone was at the rear, and no one bothered to glance back into the moldy gloom when Lina Jean's voice trembled over the swish of the washers, or when she laughed her nervous laugh. Sometimes she brought Jamie's diapers and did a few loads of wash while she made her call to David. Rita, as Lina Jean's mother liked to be called instead of Mom, didn't mind watching the baby if Lina Jean was doing something constructive like the laundry. In fact, Rita usually sent some of her uniforms along for Lina Jean to look after — gentle cycle, delicate dry, and onto hangers as quick as they dried. Rita had to have her uniforms just so because she worked with the public, she said. She ran a beauty parlor in a small trailer down the street from the larger trailer in which she and Lina Jean and the baby lived.

The best phone booth was in Blossom's Dry Goods and Drugstore, around the corner from the Pioneer Village Reconstruction. It stood inside the rear door, an old-fashioned booth with four solid wooden walls and a shelf under the phone onto which Lina Jean could stack up her quarters, or lay her shoulder bag and spiral notebook. Before she made her call, she'd buy a Coke from the machine and go over the notes she'd jotted in the blue notebook that was her journal. David had told her to keep a journal so she could chart her spiritual progress. Her spiritual development was as important to him as his own, he told her once. That was his work. He was a priest.

Sometimes she read him the notes she'd made in her journal, but usually she just read him lines she'd copied from the book he'd given her. She didn't want to take the chance of Alberta Pollack, or anyone else, overhearing anything too personal. She was having a hard time getting through the book, so she read the lines that he himself had once underlined. He underlined everything he read, he told her — yellow for agreement, blue for possible sermon material. In the margin he'd made black check marks beside the points he found especially moving or insightful. These marks had been made long before he knew her, but she thought of them as secret notes to her. She worked at the yellowed pages as though there were a message there for her in a complicated code that she must learn to break. Sometimes she wished he hadn't given her the book, it was so difficult. But that day when she had talked to him the first time, she was glad of the gift. Imagine just reaching into a bookcase, picking out a book, and giving it to an almost total stranger! It seemed a promise.

It was a hot Sunday morning in late August when she met David. She was walking Jamie in his stroller, wandering idly through town, feeling bored and lonely and disgusted with her looks, for a cold sore had formed in the corner of her mouth. Big orange butterflies shivered over the weeds and the sun was white in the pale sky. She didn't pay attention to the clapboard Catholic church, which looked more like a bungalow than a real church, until people walked out, shading their eyes with sheets of mimeographed paper that must be the programs. Practically no Catholics lived in Highwood. The only Catholic Lina Jean knew was Carmen Garcia, whose father herded sheep on the government land. In high school, Carmen had worn a thin gold chain with a delicate cross dangling at the base of her throat. Lina Jean had wanted such a chain and cross. She had been plumper then, her face even more round, her pale, fine hair dragging on her shoulders, no matter how carefully Rita waved it when it was washed. Lina Jean hoped that with a gold chain and cross she would become slim, dark, mysterious, as intensely silent as Carmen Garcia, and capable of passion. Rita gave Lina Jean a silver chain with a Peace symbol on it. It wasn't the same at all.

Most of the folks who went to the Catholic service were tourists — campers in the summer, skiers in the winter — or a few old people whose names Lina Jean didn't know. But there was also Alberta Pollack, who wore an oval blue Mary medal on her watch and taped an Advent calendar on her cash register when she put up Christmas decorations at the Mountain Inn Café. Even as Lina Jean watched over the privet hedge that separated the church from the house next to it, she saw fat, untidy Alberta come blinking out into the sun, pushing up the gray straggles at the back of her neck, and pause to speak to the young priest who stood in the shallow band of shade by the door.

Jamie whimpered and Lina Jean pushed his cuddling blanket against his cheek and rocked the stroller. She studied the priest. His curly hair was reddish brown, his short beard darker. The skin on his cheeks and forehead was pale, except for a strip of sunburn down his narrow nose. A city fellow, then. A tasseled rope held his white robe close around his slim waist, and she saw beneath the skirt the hems of black trousers and black shoes. He glanced at the people climbing into their vans and pickups; his eyes were a clear, primary blue, like poster paint.

When Alberta was out of sight, Lina Jean maneuvered Jamie's

stroller across the yellowed grass toward the church. A buzz like droning bees hummed in her head. Walking toward the handsome priest was like climbing a steep trail above the timber line: she ran out of breath and had to push herself forward.

The stroller wheels bumped the porch and Jamie let out a squeal from the jolt. The priest looked down at her and smiled. "You wouldn't park a car like that, would you?"

"I drive a school bus," she blurted. "Burton Township. K through eighth grade."

He stepped to the edge of the porch above her, his shadow shielding her eyes from the glare. "Hard work in this mountain country."

She nodded. It *was* hard work. Rita didn't understand, because Lina Jean had her hours off in the middle of the day. But often she had trouble sleeping, her shoulders ached so, and always her head hurt from concentrating on the bad roads, from the screaming kids, from worrying about being on time. "Damn hard." She was grateful that he understood. And then she blushed. You don't talk to a priest like he's one of Rita's cowboy boyfriends, she warned herself.

But he didn't seem to mind. "Were you looking for someone?" He was still smiling, his teeth as white, even, and clean as the collar he wore.

"You," she said, terrified at her boldness.

He scratched his beard. "Do I know you?"

She shook her head.

"Well, let's get that child up these steps and out of the sun. I'll slip off this hot cassock and we'll get acquainted." As he spoke, he stepped down to her and lifted the stroller with Jamie still in it up onto the porch. Then he leaned down and winked at the little boy. "Your mom thinks she's driving her bus when she pushes you. Look out." He winked at Lina Jean, too, and a sharp pain twisted just below her heart. Lord, even when they don't mean to, men make it hard on you!

She followed the priest up the center aisle of the dim church. A smear of light entered through the milky panes, and she breathed dust and a sweet scent like the strawberry incense she burned when she smoked dope and didn't want Rita to know.

"There's an office back there. Open the window. I'll be with you in a minute."

She pushed at the wooden window frame in the small, book-lined office, her hands shaking. What would happen now? She had the sensation of hurtling down an icy road, the bus rocking, out of control. To make the room stop spinning, she closed her eyes.

He was already talking as he came in behind her, something about his drive up from Denver, his car engine, the truck traffic. She didn't get the story, but he seemed to think she would know what he meant. Her hands pushed into the pockets of her jean skirt, she turned and leaned against the desk to keep her balance. Now he didn't look like a priest at all. He wore a blue-and-white-striped V-neck shirt. A narrow gold chain with an oval gold medal nested in his brown chest hair. Faintly freckled, his arms were white as winter skin. She wanted to touch the raised blue veins inside his wrists.

He motioned for her to sit down on the metal folding chair and he took the canvas chair by the desk. He smiled again. "So?"

Another blush heated her chest and the buzz became louder.

"Don't be shy," he said gently. "You're here. You came for a reason."

She looked down at her bare feet in her plastic thongs. She handed Jamie a teething biscuit.

Then he was holding his hand out to her. "Maybe we should introduce ourselves. I'm Father David Alexander. You could call me David. That seems more natural to me, though the older priests always want to be called Father."

His hand was hot but dry, his grip firm. She was glad she had wiped her own hand on her skirt after she gave Jamie the cookie. "Lina Jean Byrne," she managed. "Lina Jean's my grandma's name."

To her relief David talked for a while about the church in Highwood, explaining to her that it was a mission, really. He would come up every other week, and when winter rolled around another priest from Denver, one with a jeep, would have the responsibility. He liked Highwood, he said—clean air, the green upland meadows, the mountain peaks all around. "Do you like living here?" he asked her.

She had never asked herself that question, but now her mouth wasn't so dry, and she could answer. "It's home. That's about all you can say for it."

"Tell me about yourself, Lina Jean." His fingertips touched the back of her hand, urging her on.

"He's not legit." She gave Jamie's stroller a tug. The room was spinning again. She had said the very last thing she wanted to say!

He nodded. Maybe he didn't understand her.

"I'm not married. Never was." She wanted to run now, but her legs were shaking.

"Ah!" David squeezed Jamie's plump arm.

She rushed on with her story. "Raymond Silva was my boyfriend, I guess you'd call him. He drove through here every week with a big truckload of logs. After we got to talking that first time at the Burger Chef where I was working, he'd look me up whenever he came into town. So I went out with him. Then in a few months it turned out I was pregnant, and when I told him he drove off toward Buena Vista, and that's the last I saw of him. Now it's me and my mom and Jamie."

"A love child," David said.

In order to clarify *that* right away, she said, "I love Jamie all right, but I can't say I loved Raymond Silva. He was a good time."

David shook his head, his lips set tight, his voice firm. "I mean, you *had* the baby. That's so rare, now. You thought about the baby as well as yourself and now here's this handsome son. That's *love.*" He drew the word out like something cool and delicious and soothing on his tongue.

She hadn't thought of it that way, but she liked his version better than the truth. The truth was she had denied she *could* be pregnant until it was too late. Her fears had paralyzed her: she hadn't even had a boyfriend before; she had finally got a job; she was only eighteen; Rita would kill her. And with a kid, who would ever, ever marry her? Raymond Silva certainly wouldn't marry her. He was already married. He had a snapshot of his wife and little girl thumbtacked up next to the mattress in the sleeper behind his truck cab. She hadn't seen it the first few times, and by the time she did it had seemed childish to complain.

"Love?" she repeated after him, as though he were teaching her a new word. "It's nothing special to love your own baby."

He leaned toward her, his face tense with energy. "Oh, but it is, Lina Jean. Love is always special. It's special because God gives us the power to love. 'God is love.' You've heard that, haven't you?"

"I went to the Baptist Sunday school a few times."

"Little children learn that lesson, but sometimes we have to learn it all over again as adults. You've got a head start. If you have the power to love, you're a fortunate woman, Lina Jean. Love isn't something you can use up on just one other person, even someone as dear as your child. God gave you the power to love so you can love others, and so you can love Him."

She leaned back, trembling.

He glanced at his watch and frowned, a sharp line jagging down between his eyebrows. He was older than she had thought at first, maybe thirty, maybe even older than thirty.

"Listen," he said hurriedly. "I've got to drive down to Antero Junction for a funeral. I'm the chief circuit rider today. But I want to give you a book about a man who learned to love God. It's a story you'll like. Read it and tell me what you think, will you?" He swung around and pulled a paperback off the bookshelves behind him. Handing it to her, he explained, "I moved some of my old books in here. Don't worry about losing it. Just enjoy it."

The book lay in her lap as light as a piece of white bread.

"And tell me what you think of it?" he insisted.

She mouthed Yes.

"I have to go now, but stop by again two Sundays from today. Or better yet, call me." He scribbled numbers on a piece of paper. When he slipped the paper into the book, she thought the back of his hand brushed her thigh.

"Call you?"

"Why not? The housekeeper at the rectory will answer. Ask for Father David and tell me how you're coming with the book. I think you came here today for a reason, and we should stay in touch."

"Can you call a priest just to talk?"

"If *I* say so." He smiled, ushering her ahead of him back through the church.

Because she didn't want Rita to hear, Lina Jean saved her quarters for pay phones. She kept them in a purple felt Seagram's bag from a gift bottle of whiskey Raymond Silva had given her. At night she held the bag with its comfortable weight of quarters in her lap while she tried to read the book. But how could she concentrate? If she so much as remembered David's low, dark voice speaking her name, her face flamed, and painful threads of fire ran down her arms and into her palms. If she thought of his face when he had looked at her, saying "love," her breath was as hard to catch as though she'd been hit in the chest. When she whispered his name, cupping her hand over her mouth so Rita wouldn't hear—"David!"—she thought she would faint. He hadn't judged her for the mistake she'd made with Raymond Silva. She was clean and new and in love. Oh, she had it bad. She was a goner, and unlucky, too—first a married man, and now a Catholic priest, who could never marry her either.

The first time, she called him from the phone booth at the truck stop while she got her bus tires checked. When she heard the husky voice she had imagined so often, she started, scattering her carefully piled quarters onto the tin floor of the booth. But he made it easy for her, as he had before. "What did you do today?" he asked her. Even though she was shaking she could answer that one. No one had ever asked her about herself before. Certainly not Raymond Silva, who seemed to assume that she didn't exist when he wasn't with her.

Whenever she called David he had her begin with her day. She told him about the weather, the road conditions, a cold she was fighting off, an elk she had startled out of a creek bottom, the aspens with their gold-dollar leaves, Jamie's first words. Talking to David made her life real. Then she would say, "And I've been thinking about what you said about love." He'd take it from there. He'd quote Bible passages, his voice like silk on the solemn words. He spoke about the hand of God in the lives of men. He talked about God's love penetrating the arena of human history. As she listened, she hung on to the phone as though she were dangling off the bridge over the Royal Gorge and only David could save her life.

On every other Sunday, Lina Jean left Jamie with Rita, who didn't trust Catholics but was glad Lina Jean was getting some values pounded into her head. She went to mass, and afterward she met David for the half hour he could spare before he drove on to the next church. While she read from her journal, he ate the sandwich he had brought for his lunch, taking big, determined bites and gulping iced tea from his thermos. Then he'd talk, his short hands with blunt fingers cutting the air as he made his points about love. She imagined his hands on her throat, then unbuttoning her blouse, coming to rest on her breasts. In the cracked windowpane behind him the autumn sun sizzled like lightning.

David smiled, but he almost never laughed. She wished sometimes she could bring them some beers and slow things up so they'd have time to relax and laugh a little. He never made jokes like Raymond Silva had. You could give it to Raymond Silva for that: he knew how to make a woman laugh, him and his cheerful dirty stories. David was the deadly serious type, but maybe that's how priests should be — intense and focused on their work.

Once she asked him, "You're always asking about my daily life. What's your life like?"

"I try not to think about it," he said quickly, and she didn't ask again.

Another time she said, "You aren't at all what I thought a priest would be."

"You've hit it on the head," he told her.

When he didn't say any more, she urged, "I mean, you pay such close attention. And why do you pay attention to *me*? I'm not even a Catholic." Of course she had hoped he would say, I love you, Lina Jean.

He had finished his lunch and was fitting the lid back on the plastic sandwich box. He didn't look up. "You want to learn what I've got to teach." Then he changed the subject. "Saint Benedict was a genius, you know that? Way back in the sixth century he knew more about what makes a man tick than any of the bishops do today."

"What's that mean?"

"The Benedictine brothers lived in a community. They had to obey the rules of their community, and if one of them broke the rules, he was sent away. That makes sense, doesn't it?"

She nodded.

"The brother had to go and live on the hillside and ponder his mistake. He might decide to repent and come back, he might decide to leave for good. Fair enough. But now here's where Benedict's genius came in. He said that another brother must go and stay with the exile until the exile had made his decision. The exile must not be abandoned. He *must* have the comfort of human love." He glanced up at her, his eyes as blue as the eastern sky at sunset. "That's another aspect of love, Lina Jean. To stand between a man and the void in his self. Do you understand me?"

She nodded again, because she knew he wanted her to. But to tell the truth, she didn't understand. His face was both pale and angry as he spoke, and she thought of an electric fence: if she touched him a current would crack through her body and she would be frayed and burned, by what power she didn't know, but not by love — of that much she was sure.

"You're coming back here, aren't you?" Why had she asked him that?

"Sure." The furrow deepened between his eyes. "I pull in here right on time, don't I? Just like you in your school bus. The bishop thinks all his priests are like buses. We don't have feelings or needs. But there are some of us who don't see it that way."

A tremor that reminded her of her baby's first stirrings inside her womb made her voice shrivel. "What do you mean?"

"God knows." He shoved his mouth into a lopsided smile. "*I* don't." Then he asked about her journal, so she couldn't tell him that she was scared and didn't even know if she was frightened for herself or for him. But after all, nothing changed; she called him twice a week for a few minutes and saw him every other Sunday, and sooner than she would have guessed she finished his book. When she returned it, he didn't offer her another. Later, she thought that had been a sign.

The second Sunday in December was scheduled to be David's last mass in Highwood until spring. She waited in the office for him with the Christmas gift she'd bought him tucked in her shoulder bag. It was an expandable watchband with real Zuni turquoise decoration. It had cost too much, but she wanted to give him something wonderful, something no one had given him before.

When he came into the office, he was pulling on a heavy gray sweater. His hair was tousled and he was frowning. "Don't they have heat here? We could pull up some pews and burn them, I guess. Aren't you cold?"

"I kept my coat on."

At the window he looked out into the powdery snow being lifted by the wind like spray from water.

She had her speech rehearsed. "Listen, David? I was wondering. I mean, you're not going to be up here again for a long time. Can I keep calling you? I want to. I could even take the Greyhound down into Denver some Sunday . . ." Her voice ran down, like one of Jamie's windup toys whining to a halt. She had asked for too much.

His back still to her, he said quietly, "I won't be there."

"What?"

He swung around, blinking from the fierce light off the snow, and flung himself into the canvas chair. "I'm leaving."

"Leaving? Going where?" Through the stirrings of panic she hurriedly tried to calculate how much it would cost to call him in California, say, or New York.

"Just leaving. I'm not sure yet where we'll end up. Where we can get jobs, I guess."

"We? A bunch of you?"

He slid his hands deep into the pockets of his black trousers. "No, just me and Ann. We're going to be married."

She heard herself repeat, "Ann?" The name was as meaningless as a nonsense word from a nursery rhyme.

"Ann Eveland. She was a nun, Sacred Heart. We love each other. It seems there's no room for human love inside the Church. Just the love of God. For some that's not enough."

A wave of pure pain battered her heart. "Ann," she repeated, although her voice wasn't her own; it came out shrill and thin.

"You'd like Ann, Lina Jean. She's very kind and warm —"

"Ann!" So all that time he had talked so passionately of love he was really talking about this Ann! He wasn't thinking about God. He wasn't thinking about her, Lina Jean Byrne. He'd been justifying himself, thinking of reasons why he should leave to be with that nun.

"Don't —"

"David!" she cried in that queer, high voice.

She heard, more than felt, her knees hit the bare wood floor, and suddenly she was kneeling in front of him, reaching for his legs. With both hands he made a quick gesture for her to stand, but she couldn't.

He was on his feet, looking past her toward the door. Behind her in the open doorway stood Alberta Pollack, carrying one of her homemade Christmas wreaths.

"Just a moment," David said to Alberta.

Then, as though Lina Jean had knelt before him for his blessing, he whispered to her, "Go in peace," and his hot thumb traced the sign of the cross on her forehead.

Lina Jean pulled up the hood of her parka, grabbed her shoulder bag, and pushed past Alberta, who blocked the door with her spray of ribboned pine. Just get out, get out of there before she cried. As the side door creaked open and she ran out into the blowing snow, she heard David call, "Will you wait?" But what was there left to say?

Still, with the unreasonable hope that he might come back, she went to mass two Sundays later. A heavy-set, white-headed priest in after-ski boots was there in David's place. In his talk the priest compared life to the Rose Bowl game and Jesus to a winning quarterback. After that she didn't go back to church. But of course she had to go on making phone calls at regular intervals. If she stopped making the calls, everyone in town would know she didn't have a man anymore. Once a week she forced herself to use a phone where she knew she'd be seen. The Mountain Inn Café was the best place for this, and now that Alberta thought that Lina Jean was a convert, she smiled instead of staring. Often Lina Jean just dialed the weather service and listened to the tape several times through. If she knew that Rita was at the beauty parlor, she dialed their home phone and let it ring and ring and ring. Once she called United Dial-a-Prayer in Denver, her hand shaking with memory as she thrust in her money. As soon as she had dialed she knew she had made a mistake, but before she could hang up she heard what she was almost sure was David's recorded voice say, as huskily as a lover's, "In this cold season, let our love —"

The Cat Who Fought the Rain

I'm crossing the parking lot behind my post office when I see the
storm coming in from the west, cumulus high, bruised purple mountains. Before I climb into my Pontiac I feel thunder in the ground.
I'm sensitive that way: I could pick up artillery just like I was getting personal messages. And why not? I read that some folks get
migraines just before volcanoes erupt. Across the street, the birches
in front of the Wisconsin State Building twist and thrash. Inside out,
the leaves are silvery fish scales. The girl waiting on the bus stop
there tries to hold down her denim skirt, but it tangles up over her
knees. When she bends to grab it, her backpack slips down her arm.
Some papers fall out of the pack and blow like the leaves. I pull
up beside her. "Want a ride?" I yell over the wind.

While she's figuring what do I have in mind, I'm enjoying her
blonde hair blowing across her face. She gets a strand out of her
mouth to ask, "Do I know you? I don't have my contacts in."

"Sure, you know me. I deliver mail."

"Oh, hi, then!" Like now we've been introduced properly.

"It's gonna storm."

"Where you headed?"

"Out Old Sauk toward Black Earth."

The wind lifts her hair straight back like wheat. Grit bites the sides
of my car.

"I guess I could get out at Gammon Road." She opens the door
and pushes her backpack in ahead of her. I see she's got a ruffly

white petticoat on under the skirt, and real cowboy boots, the kind
with fancy stitching and pointy toes.

"Thought I was going to get soaked." She waves ahead of us to
the wall of rain coming across the golf course.

"Summer's over. When you work outside, you notice the seasons."
I pull out into traffic and get stopped right away by the light. That
gives me a chance to smile at her and to notice that her tan is nice
and even on her shoulders, and just as even through all the holes
in her eyelet blouse.

"Anyway, summer was boring." She gets out a comb and goes to
work untangling all that hair.

The light changes and I jam it to the floor and shoot onto University, heading west. "What did you do so boring?"

"I was lifeguarding at this private pool where my mom moved.
It's mostly older people, so nobody swims. I read a lot."

"Didn't save any lives?"

"Only my own. My big achievement was to teach Nicky to swim.
He's my stepbrother by my mom's second marriage. A pain in the
neck."

I roll down my window so I can feel the first rain on my bare arm.
The smell of dust and cut grass billows ahead of the storm. The alder
copse beside the road bends toward us in the wind. If there was a
man in those trees I could spot him: a man doesn't move when the
trees do. You look for the still place and you're right on him.

"So, you're a mailman?"

"Nope, I'm a fireman disguised in this blue stuff."

She laughs to be polite. A lady's pulling sheets off her line when
the rain reaches her. She puts her arms over her head and runs. I
turn onto Old Sauk and the storm hits us.

"Hey!" the girl yells, and I roll up my window. "Tidal wave!"

Heat steams from the pavement and the rain hammers on us. I
turn the washers to high, but it doesn't help much. In less than a
minute I can't see five feet ahead. "I'm pulling over," I tell her, and
ease into the parking lot of Knoches Food Center. "Hope you're not
in a hurry."

"Just going home." But she looks cross, like maybe there's some
guy waiting for her.

I lean back and scratch my beard. She's a pretty girl, and I'm not sorry to be stuck with her for a few minutes. "How about some tunes?" I switch on the radio, wishing I could still use dope, so we could share a J.

"Ninety-two?"

"You got it." But I'm dialing mostly static.

She's chewing on her finger. "Listen, I wasn't hitching. I was waiting for a bus."

"I know that."

"I *don't* hitch."

"Didn't think so." I wonder if her eyes are so blue when she's not tan.

"Okay, then." She touches the knob and country-and-western music blasts. "You were almost on it."

"Nice job." I turn the volume down and realize that, son-of-a-bitch, it's good old Lila, singing her latest hit single, "My broken heart's only your broken toy." A solid sheet of water's running down the windshield. "Go for it, Lila." I give her the thumbs-up.

"You like Lila Kane?" The girl taps her foot in those expensive boots.

"Her real name's Lila Kaminsky."

She cocks her head, paying attention, now. "You read that?"

"She's married to my pop." I close my eyes and lay my head back, enjoying myself.

After a moment, she says, "I don't believe you."

"Well, she is." I don't look, but I can feel her looking me over real good, figuring my age about thirty and way too old to have Lila Kane for my mom. Then I turn my head, wink at her, and she blushes.

"So, my stepmother's Lila Kane, what do you think of that?"

"Big talk, and how would you prove it?" But I see she believes me. If you look a girl straight in the eye, she'll believe you. Anyway, it's the truth.

"Like I said, her real name's Kaminsky, a nice Polish name, but no kind of label for a country-western singer with sequins on her jeans. Pop came up with Kane. Our name's Piper."

She's interested now; I knew she'd be. Everybody thinks show biz

is something. Lila's cut is over and Willie Nelson's on. The rain lets
up a little; I see other cars around us in the lot, waiting.

"She makes big money, I bet."

"Oh, yeah. Lila does just fine."

"Your dad in music, too?"

"He sets up stock car races. He's always asking me to come with
him, but I can't get into that. Pop says that when he sees those cars
come streaming across the fields toward the racetrack, plumes of
dust spouting up behind them, he wants to cry. That's what he says.
'It damn near makes me cry, Mark. You should come on board.' "

She's chewing on her fingernail again, her teeth small and even.
"More fun than delivering mail."

"I like my job. Sure is better than farming, anyway, which is what
Pop did before he got this idea about stock cars."

"That where your real mom is—back on the farm?"

The worst of the rain is over. I start up the engine and ease through
the deep runoff at the curb. The other cars nose in behind me, waiting to see if I make it. I make it. "My real mom's dead."

"Oh."

So as not to stop conversation right there, I ask her, "You work
around here, then?"

"Well, that lifeguarding job's over now. I'm going into dental
hygiene. Registration is Monday." She crosses her legs and leans to
wipe her boots with a tissue. When her blouse gaps at the top, I catch
a glimpse of a bra the same color as her tan.

Her name's inked on the side of her backpack: Betsy Doyle.

"Betsy, do you like Chinese food?" I was thinking how good some
would taste.

"At Ruby Lee's, you mean? That's my favorite." She leans against
the door so she can look at me.

"Why not? Your mom expecting you home for supper?"

"I moved out when she got married again. I've got my own place."

"Ruby Lee's, then?"

"The thing is, I've got to go to my place to look after my cat. He's
just a baby. Last night he cried all night long."

So I stop at Ruby's and get a carton of egg rolls, another of chicken and pea pods, and an order of those spare ribs to go, and we drive to Betsy's place to look after her cat.

She's got one of those one-room efficiencies, but not bad — posters on the walls, plants in baskets, some wicker chairs she probably got from her mom's porch, a sofa that folds out into a bed. In the middle of the square of blue linoleum in front of the stove, a scrawny kitten is looking up at us.

"There's my big boy!"

Girls talk to cats the same as they do to babies. City girls, not country girls. Mom, or my sister, Jessie, would yell at a cat like they'd yell at me. And we weren't really farmers at all, just trying to be. We learned right away not to sweet-talk animals, though.

When she holds the kitten up to her cheek, a ribbon of her hair falls against the fur — same taffy color. I figure I'm supposed to notice that, so I say, "Pretty picture."

Betsy's sure pretty enough — her arms have a baby-oil shine when she raises the kitten for me to see — but that *cat*. He's a runt, skinny and wet-looking, with big, hungry eyes in his flat face, and way too young to leave his momma.

"What's this dude's name?" I touch the kitten's head and feel bones small as a squirrel's.

She growls at him. "Tiger."

"Tiger!" I have to smile at that skimpy cat with his feet dangling through her fingers.

"It just fits so perfectly to his stripy colors."

Since drug rehab, I don't remember things good, but I wish I could get a hold on why that name makes me want to cry.

"Give your kitten his supper, then, and I'll set ours out."

She gets a carton of milk from the fridge, and a big jug of white wine. "Choose a place."

I've already got one chosen — that coffee table in front of the sofa that folds out into a bed.

While we're eating, my mind jumps around. I keep pouring us more wine, and Betsy's telling me her story, but I'm paying just enough attention so I can say "nice going," or "sounds good" when she leaves a pause. Mostly I'm thinking about my sister, Jessie, though I can't figure why.

I plainly see me and Jessie riding our bikes up and down the gravel roads around our farm, just up and back, because there was no place to ride *to*. We were missing Chicago—delis, movies, buses, bowling alleys, our playground by school. Pop had this idea we were going to have a simple country life, clean living and all. He'd got caught making book in the back room of our grocery store, and decided to start fresh. Jess and I hated it.

She used to ride at me head-on, full-speed on her blue Schwinn, rump high, her coppery braids flying out behind and her teeth gritted in her warrior grin. Who'd dodge first! I always did. Even though I'm two years older, I was scared of her. I knew she'd just as soon barrel into me as not. It would have been something to do on those everlasting days when there was nothing to do. She didn't have the same grasp of the consequences as I did—nothing to do *and* a cast on my arm? No way. I'd swerve, and she'd shout, "Chicken!"

"You want this last sweet-n-sour?" Betsy gets my attention by holding the packet out to me.

I put it on my plate, then I take her hand and lick the sweet off her pinky with the gold initial ring. She's a nice girl; I lucked out this time.

"You probably got a boyfriend, a cute girl like you."

"Oh, *him*. He thinks all there is to life is working at Radio Shack. I'm more or less through with him." She licks off the rest of her fingers, her face all rosy from that wine. She's slipped off her boots, and her bare toes are tan, too.

"Betsy Doyle," I say real slowly, so I'll remember. She likes that. I pour her some more wine and we finish up the spare ribs, me paying close attention to her family stories this time around.

After we eat, she gets some grass from a sandwich bag in her desk drawer and rolls a J. I say, "Not me." She doesn't have so much to say, now. She just smokes.

After a while she asks, "You want music?" But it's nice and peaceful in her place, the rain soft and steady on the panes, so I shake my head.

"You're so damned pretty," I tell her. "This Radio Shack guy's a fool."

She arches her back. "Mark, do you know you are just so *nice*?"

By now, I'm figuring that the plaid blanket spread on the floor, with some of those big pillows, would be cosier than hefting out the bed. More subtle, too.

But I don't have to plan. Some girls get so nervous, wondering when you're going to move on them, that they jump the gun and start things off themselves. Just so they'll *know*. Betsy's one of those. All of a sudden, she's on my lap, trying to show me everything she's ever learned all at once.

I slide down onto the floor, pull her down between my legs, and organize her some. "One thing at a time, Betsy Doyle." Then I kiss her, and dish it out to her real slow, the way I like it. And I make sure she likes it that way, too.

The room's dark, Waylon Jennings's playing on a stereo in another apartment, and Betsy's gone to sleep on her stomach, one foot on top of the other. I like the pale marks where her bathing suit was, especially her sweet, pale cheeks, but I pull a crocheted afghan over her so she doesn't chill. When I lean up to get my smokes from my shirt pocket, the kitten jumps onto my bare stomach — claws and damp fur. Tiger!

One thing I learned from Pop is that if you write something down, you don't have to worry about it anymore; he was a great one for lists. So I get my notebook from my shirt pocket, too, and write down *the cat who liked to fight the rain*. Now I can forget about that cat.

Except that I can't. Sometimes a memory lodges in you like a shred of metal, and you worry it, even though it hurts, hoping it'll work itself out again. I got our old tabby, Tiger, on my mind now, his namesake turning around in my chest hair to make himself a bed where he won't be lonesome.

On the farm, one thing we had was lots of cats. Most were barn cats that we'd pitch off the back porch the way we threw the soft-ball, underhand, but hard. Jessie complained, "Why do we get all these dumb cats? Cats who don't even know how to *be* cats? How come this one thinks he's got to fight with water?" She shagged a peach pit at the tabby sitting just behind the gutter downspout, swiping at the running water with unsheathed claws. The cat snapped those sharp teeth at the drops that spattered onto the chipped green paint of the porch.

I thought maybe cats were evolving into a different breed, a more aggressive strain coming along. We were studying evolution in junior high, and anything seemed possible. I was the one who named that tabby Tiger.

"Jess, what if this dumb-ass cat *wins*? What are you gonna say then?"

"You aren't supposed to say 'dumb-ass.' " Jess started in on another peach. I wasn't, but I knew she liked it; all kids like words you aren't supposed to say. Sometimes I made up nonsense words and told her they were dirty; she got just as big a kick out of those as from the real ones.

Jess flicked a pebble at the cat. It winced and hissed without turning from the rain. "Water *always* wins." Maybe, after all, she was the logical one; I was the dreamer. "Look at floods. Storms. Stuff like hurricanes."

"I'm putting money on this cat," I told her.

Tiger got hit by a car. In fact, Mom hit him one morning when she was backing out of the barn to drive into Sauk City where she taught high school. I was upstairs getting dressed and saw her flatten Tiger when he jumped for her rear wheels. She got out of the car real matter-of-fact, picked up old Tiger, and laid him on the compost heap. It came to me that she'd adjusted to farm life better than the rest of us. That was why, when Pop left us and took up with Lila and her cowboy sidemen, Mom stayed on there.

I lean over and kiss the top of Betsy's head, right on that place that's supposed to be soft when you're born, and smell her honey shampoo. Maybe she'll wake up so I can hold her. But she doesn't. She rubs her nose with her fist and curls up on her side, her back to me. That's some better, anyway. Me and Tiger ease up against her warm rump. I'm thinking that's how life is: I need to hold her, but what one person needs the other can't even guess.

I can still reach my notebook. I write down *Gardels,* because

Mom's maiden name just came to me. They always ask you that for passports and such and I draw a blank. I can get hold of scenes, like movies with no sound track, but a whole lot of words are just gone.

Mom's name is written in the front of that book of hers I kept because she was reading it so often toward the end.

They let me out of the drug rehab program to come home; Mom had been sick before I went to Nam, but she was much, much worse. Jess said it wasn't long now. Histoplasmosis — we figured she got the fungus in her lungs from looking after the chickens in their moldy coop — our clean, new country life. Jess was staying with Mom and was up all night, most nights. She called me in Tellurian and got me out to come help.

Jess did days, I did nights; I hadn't been sleeping so good, anyway. I didn't mind sitting up with Mom, reading to her or listening to the radio. They'd got a hospital bed and oxygen tank in the back bedroom that had been Mom and Pop's. Mom could take off her oxygen mask to talk. She was a tall, red-headed woman, with soft, heavy arms, but, by the time I got home, it seemed she'd got small, mostly skin and bones. Freckles everywhere, though, like I remembered. Her brown eyes were bigger than ever. I imagined her looking right through me, like an X ray into my head.

When she coughed, she spit up shreds of her lungs. I wiped blood from her mouth and some from the margin of the book she was reading, an old poetry anthology with water stains on the cover; on the front page, *Mary Gardels, Ball State Teachers College.*

"Want me to read to you, Mom?"

She handed me the book and I gave her a few lines where she pointed.

> I walk through the long schoolroom questioning;
> A kind old nun in a white hood replies.

Marking the place, I said, "You thinking about your teaching, aren't you?"

She shook her head.

I said the title, "Among School Children."

She took off her mask. "Love poem." A rasp more than words.

"Love?" I looked closer. "Whereabouts?"

She pushed her forefinger at some lines farther down the page.

> And thereupon my heart is driven wild:
> She stands before me as a living child.

She took a breath of oxygen. "Driven *wild*."

"So, it's a love poem?"

"Yes." She put the mask on and lay back to rest.

I wondered if Mom had loved Pop. I don't mean in the last few years when he was smashing stock cars and then chasing Lila. I mean when they were young. He had black hair and good, broad shoulders —those snaps of him holding me and Jessie on the swimming dock, us kids squinting into the sun and Pop standing real straight so his stomach wouldn't make folds. Had she loved him then?

It was risky to ask. "Thinking about Pop?"

"No. About love. You keep. Wanting." She looked at me so helplessly that I looked away from those deep-seeing eyes. Right that moment I wished I was back in those blank, mellow days on Methadone.

I guess she didn't want me to dwell on the thought of a woman longing for love right while she was dying, so she motioned for me to open the window wider. The steady rain had brought up the smells of mint run wild in the kitchen garden and the tomatoes we'd forgot to pick. I changed channels on the little tv until I got an old Spencer Tracy movie. With the sound off, it didn't bother Mom.

After a long time, she wrote on her pad and passed it to me: *I wish I hadn't killed your cat.*

"What cat?"

The one that liked rain. She looked steadily at me over the edge of the mask.

"Oh, hell, Mom. We had tons of cats. Anyway, he didn't *like* the rain. He hated it. He and the rain were enemies. It was just that water didn't scare him like it did the others. He was a dumb, fearless old cat, Mom. He jumped right at your tires. Don't think about him."

I was going to go on and tell her that many times I'd kicked that cat off the porch like he was a football, just to watch him land on his feet and race off, spitting. I decided not to go that far.

He had a name. At least that's what I think she wrote; her writing was awful spidery and the pencil needed sharpening.

I went off to sharpen it and to see if Jess remembered that cat's name. She was asleep, flung out on her bed, but still wearing the blouse and jeans she'd worn all day; those days we just dove into sleep when we could.

And when I came back to Mom's room, she was asleep, too. I straightened up her sheet and saw that she was about as peaceful as she could get. I wondered when she'd want another shot. Then I fell asleep watching Spencer.

When I woke again, around 4:00 A.M., I knew Mom was dead. There was no sound at all, that's how. Just the wind in the corn and trucks out on the highway. I wish I'd thought "Mom," but instead I thought, "body bag." I'm not ashamed; you don't have control over thoughts.

I woke Jessie and she cried. But I didn't. I called up Pop in Chicago. Lila answered. I like Lila well enough, except right then I hated her.

"Tell Pop that my mom is dead."

Lila went "huh!" like I'd kicked her in the stomach. Maybe I had. But she's my age, and I figured she could take care of herself. You always think someone your own age can get along all right; it's the older or younger ones you worry about.

I hung up before she could answer.

Jess phoned Tim, her husband, and then we had some brandy. I sat out on the porch in the swing, watching the rain, waiting until it got light and someone would already be awake when I called the funeral home. By then I'd remembered that cat's name. Too late.

I wake with the kitten's claws in my shoulder, his teeth in my chin. "Whoa!" I whisper. Maybe I rolled on him. Betsy's still asleep, a soft snore on every other breath. Allergies, I guess. I pull away from her, holding the kitten real careful so he'll calm down. I sit up and pull on my shirt and pants. The lighted dial on my watch reads 12:32. It looks like Betsy's going to sleep on her blanket all night, so I fold her skirt and blouse for her and cover her good with the afghan.

In the kitchen I toss the empty cartons into the trash, wipe the table, and lay out things for her breakfast—the box of cereal, a bowl and spoon, coffee cup in a saucer—to get her off to a good start in the morning. Then I write her a note, tear it out of my notebook, and put it right on top of her plate where she can't miss it.

Dear Betsy,
I am holding your cat hostage.
If you want him back you'll have
to call me. 833-7049
          Mark   XXXOOO

Outside, the sky is clear now, the moon shining into all the big puddles left by the storm. A shadow scoots by us—a gray cat out hunting in the low hedges around the apartment building.

"See, you got a lot to look forward to," I tell the kitten. "Big times ahead, kiddo." Holding him close, I head for my car.

The Geese at Presque Isle

"Why not, Raker? Just tell me plainly why not?" One hand on her hip, the phone cradled against her breast, his wife stood in the doorway to the kitchen. Her shadow stretched to where he lay on the sofa in the darkened living room.

He shook his head again, wondering if the woman on the other end of the line could hear his wife's heart beating.

"You're driving there anyway!"

"By myself."

"It would be easy as pie to take her."

He sat up and scrubbed at his head, pushed his fingers through his stiff hair. "Lay off, Margie."

"You've been short-tempered lately. I'm not asking much."

"I'm trying to watch this football game!"

She squinted at him. The kitchen light outlined her metallic hair, back-lit, gray as a gull's wing. When it had started to turn — she only thirty then and on her third pregnancy — she'd said, "Dyeing is dying," and let the gray show. "You've known Flora Higbee since you were a kid." She spoke softly, but each word stood out.

"Baby-sitting," he said, more to argue than anything else. Margie made a damned career out of helping their friends. "I don't run a sheltered shop."

"No fair! She's only half-blind."

"Half-strike, whole-strike."

She took a breath. "If you're driving to Cleveland on the exact same day Flora's taking a bus there, why couldn't she go with you? All you'd have to do is drop her where she's going."

"And be late at the plant."

"Consultants don't punch time clocks."

Jamming his flannel shirt down into his jeans, he stood and strode to the picture window. At eye level a pockmark made by Mike's BB gun radiated a star of light from the streetlamp. He was stuck, and he knew it. She knew it, too.

"It's only a couple hours drive."

He shrugged, then. He'd never had a choice; about most things you don't get a choice. Think you do, but no.

Margie settled the phone back under her chin and turned away. "Flora? He says he'd be real pleased to have your company. That's 6:30 tomorrow morning. He prides on being on time."

He tested the pane with his fingertips, feeling the autumn chill. On the horizon, as if riding on the band of low, purple clouds, a ragged V of canvasbacks headed south.

He lay on the sofa again, his parka over him for a blanket. From the kitchen, Margie called, "You're a better guy than you let on, Raker Jordan." Through his half-closed eyes he watched her wipe her hands on her jeans and go back to frying chicken. In a few minutes the kids would be home, exploding into the house with their friends, cranking their music high, leaving their coats and shoes where they fell. He pushed the top of his head up against the rough tweed upholstery, made a fist, and shoved it against his lips. There's nothing to say that's worth the saying.

Morning. Hungover, as he'd been lately, he stayed in the shower a long time, thinking without remorse that he was using all the hot water. As he shaved he heard his kids' alarms going off. Cheap construction—the walls thin, the rooms few. He'd been proud when they'd bought the place, but with their second child they'd filled it, and, with the youngest, Paul, they were like sardines.

"Dad!" Nan, at the door. She washed her hair every morning, then bent forward, her blond hair dripping, to blow it dry. The bathroom smelled always of balsam now. Sixteen, and all her time went to take care of herself. In a few years she'd have kids and let herself go. "You've been in there forever!"

"I live here, too."

"You've been in there so long that Paul couldn't wait. He's peeing off the back porch and Mom's yelling at him."

In the hall, Raker passed Mike, who carried his cereal bowl and toast into the room he shared with Paul. "Morning," Raker said, but Mike just grimaced. He was a senior and had quit talking to grown-ups; grown-ups corrupted the minds of youth. He wanted to be a major league star. Who didn't?

Barefoot and in his pajamas, squatting behind the kitchen table, Paul hid from Margie. She was yelling, "Never do that!"

"Dad made me!" Dodging her slap, he bolted across the kitchen.

The same every morning. Then suddenly one day they'd be gone, even Paul.

Margie went back to making their lunches, her hair matted on the side from sleeping pressed up against Raker's back, as she always did. A casserole was defrosting by the sink. Tonight must be her bowling league at the credit union where she worked.

He filled his thermos with coffee, put a couple of extra styrofoam cups into a bag, then made two bologna sandwiches. If Flora didn't bring a snack he'd have to buy her one. Save where you could.

"Be nice to her," Margie said.

"As if I wouldn't?"

As he went out the door she made a kissing sound. He did, too. So much for that.

Streaks of sun bannered the wet grass, and a rime of ice coated the puddles in the gravel drive. The chill cleared his head. He drove across town to Flora's house — off the beltline, Margie said, by the bus stop. A friend of his oldest sister's, Flora had been four years ahead of him in school. Then in high school she'd got some disease — measles, was it? — that left her partially blind. Now she made phone solicitations for Homecrafters; she'd never married.

Her house was a yellow brick, no uglier than the others on the block. A grain elevator cast a long, blue shadow across her front yard. She already waited for him on her front porch. Wearing a tan raincoat, her canvas satchel slung over her shoulder, she looked alertly ahead into space, her head back-tilted, like a woman examining herself in a looking glass.

Pulling up at her curb, he honked. When he saw the sound had started her down the steps, he jumped from his van. She'd fall; it'd be his fault.

She met him on the poured concrete squares that formed the walk. "I can see light and dark," she said by way of greeting. "I can clearly see your shape and the shape of your car. Please don't take my arm. I do better on my own."

He stepped aside and she went ahead of him, her loafers slapping on her heels. He hadn't exchanged more than a few sentences with her in maybe twenty years, but now he was reminded of her daunting manner. She liked throwing a challenge. Staying close behind, he wondered if it was too late to say good morning.

She waited by the van. Her dark eyes were unclouded but focused somewhere beyond him. "This wasn't my idea, I want you to know that."

He opened the door for her. "It's fine."

"It's not fine."

"I mean by me."

"I doubt that. I don't mind the bus, you know."

She climbed into the front seat, pushing her satchel ahead of her. Her plaid skirt fanned over her thin legs. She wore navy blue knee socks like Nan's.

He pulled himself in on his side. "I like company."

"I don't."

He put the van in gear, eased forward onto the asphalt. "Look, Flora, would you rather take the bus?"

"Would *you* rather I did?" She sat with her chin lifted, her gaze sliding sternly past his, her close-cropped hair a salt-and-pepper cap.

Swearing to himself, he gunned to the corner. No matter where you stepped she laid a trap. "If you're going to be so damned sharp, yes, I'd rather put you on the bus."

To his surprise, she smiled, the same kind of taunting grin Paul had given his mother when he'd teased her into swatting at him that morning.

"So what'll it be?" he pressed her.

"I'd like a cup of Margie's good coffee I smell."

At the stop sign he poured them each a cupful, the steam rising like off a warm pond at evening. He worked up a little spit and took

two more aspirin. She gazed down into her cup as if she could see
as well as anybody. Better.

"I'm comfortable now," she said after a few swallows.

"This is your idea of comfort?"

"Better, anyway. I'm having a hard time lately with manners."

"We need 'em."

"Yes and no. Fictions wear me out."

"Fictions?"

"Play-acting. 'Hello, how are you?' As if anyone cared."

"So how would you have it instead?"

"Straight."

"Forget it. Nothing runs without grease."

"I'm experimenting with truth."

"Hard work, Flora."

She handed him her coffee cup in order to shrug out of her coat.
Under, she wore a plaid jumper and a white turtleneck. No tits to
speak of.

"This straight-talking business something new you're inventing?"
He wondered what he was in for today.

She leaned over her satchel. With her straight nose and blunt jaw,
she made him think more of a boy than of a woman. "Remember
I gave you a chance to put me on the bus."

"It's not gonna be as bad as all that." Though maybe it was. Anyway, it was too late now to worry about it.

He dialed in the music-and-news station and settled down for the
drive. After a few miles he noticed she'd shut her eyes, and he glanced
at her more openly. He could almost get back his boyhood memory
of her as the spunky tomboy with auburn braids who'd helped build
their tree house. Once, on a dare, she'd carried him piggyback up
the ladder to it. Then she'd got sick. Such things happened — could
happen to anyone.

Could easily happen to his Paul, for instance, who had asthma.
Often Raker had held him over the toilet, his small stomach cramp-
ing. The boy's heart thrummed like a bird beating up frantically as
he vomited and vomited mucus and couldn't be stopped. Many times
he'd been hospitalized. In the vast, dark lake of those nights, Paul
struggling for breath, tubes in his wrists and the oxygen tent over,

Raker thought so this is what it comes down to, reaching under the tent to touch the boy's heavy, damp head and his fragile throat.

Medicine couldn't do everything. There were threats everywhere. Don't think about it.

But you couldn't choose what came into your mind. Even that morning, as he watched his womanly daughter pull on her sweater, he'd thought suddenly of when she was small and he'd changed her diaper. Of her mysterious parts as perfectly bivalved as a clam shell. He wouldn't want anyone to know he remembered that picture.

Or that he thought often, even after all these years, of a confession Margie had made to him on their honeymoon. In a ma-and-pa motel out in Colorado, her head on his shoulder, the pressure of her breasts on his arm, she'd confessed that Bob Archer, Raker's best friend, had told her, "You've got a great ass, Margie." Why did that still hurt? And why should one of his strongest memories of his wife be what another guy had said to her?

Beside him, Flora sat with her chin raised, lips parted, like a singer waiting for the gesture from a choir director that would begin her song.

The highway swung north through fields of bleached corn. The reflection of sun off the hood made Raker's eyes tear and his fingers ached from caffeine. He pulled into a truck stop. He wanted a drink, but you couldn't be thinking that way in the morning.

"I'll treat you to a piece of pie," he told Flora.

"Where are the restrooms?"

He led her around to the side of the cash register, considered waiting for her, but decided she could find her own way. She'd told him twice now not to take her arm.

These places all smelled the same—stale smoke, coffee, gravy. He found a booth by the window, ordered two apple pies and two milks. He took off his glasses, cleaned them with a paper napkin, then wet the napkin in his water glass and rubbed his face. Now that he wasn't driving he felt his exhaustion. If he put his head down on the table he'd sleep at once. The sun pouring through the streaked window warmed his arms and shoulders. His hands lay on the formica table in front of him like gloves someone had left behind. Blunt fingers, raised veins, stains under his cracked nails—he'd never worn a wedding band—sissy. Ginger hairs thick on his wrists and fingers. "Paws," Nan said. "Dad, you have bear paws." Sometimes his shadow going ahead of him did remind him of a bear's—sloping shoulders, the slow gait. Too heavy—he should knock off a few pounds.

Flora slid onto the plastic bench across from him. She'd brushed her hair with water, drops clinging to her temples. She smiled toward where she must have seen his shape. Her forehead was freckled, like a pear.

"Where are you going today, Raker?"

"Anywhere you need to be."

"I mean where are you working?"

A waitress with lavender hair brought their pie and milk. When she handed Raker a bill, he saw she'd drawn a smiling face on it under the total. He stuffed it in his pocket.

"Margie said you were consulting at some steel plant."

He thought, which lie? To hell with it. He took a deep breath, as though he were flinging off the old quarry cliff into the lake. "I'm not working."

The thin skin around her large eyes puckered. "Margie—"

"I lied to her."

Her opened hands paused over her plate. She bent toward him as though she were finding him with an infra-red hunting scope, sighting more by heat than movement.

"This is your straight talk, Flora."

"I don't understand."

"The plants where I consult have all cut back, laid off, shut down. I haven't had a job in two months, can't find one." Because she couldn't see him, he didn't bother to keep the anger from his face.

"You haven't told Margie?"

"I tell her some city, Cleveland, say. Then I drive off on a Monday morning like always. Mostly I go up to the lake shore, pull into a park campground, and walk. Just walk. I've been studying the ducks and geese. Towards the end of the week, I drive on back, take some more money out of our savings, go home. They're about gone."

She let her breath out long and slow. "You could get another job, surely."

"Tell me about it."

She sipped her milk, a line of white staying in the faint down on her upper lip. "Why haven't you told Margie?"

"Because then I'd have to stay home." He could imagine that well enough, the house empty, him doing the laundry or whatever while Margie worked. This way he could still get on the road. As if he were going somewhere.

"You could—"

"I'm stopped dead in my tracks. It'll get worse and no way in the world is it going to get better."

"You're only forty, Raker."

"Eat your pie."

She cut a piece with the side of her fork, guided it to her lips, then set it back on her plate. "You wish you hadn't told me, don't you?"

"Is that a question?"

"Yes."

"I don't know."

"Believe it or not, I understand."

He got to his feet. Her and her understanding. He was sick of women understanding things—so quick and easy—as though all it took to know was saying you did. "Okay, you understand. Now you can quit. I'm going to buy a paper. You eat your pie. Then I'll drop you where you're going."

He wanted a drink, wanted to head out to that spit of land he remembered up near Erie, as good a place as any to watch geese. To be alone, nothing to explain, no one asking questions.

After a few minutes she fumbled on her coat, joined him by the cash register while he peeled off a couple of bills. He was in a hurry now. He walked ahead of her to the door, knowing she'd follow, but he took her arm to lead her across the parking lot. Before she pulled from his grip, he felt her arm as slim and muscular as a girl's.

A light wind came up and dust blew from the gravel, stinging his hands. Her coat opened like a cape, or spread wings flapping. Her hair lifted from her broad forehead to expose a line of white along her brow. He took her thin wrist, hard, to lead her around a semi. If she fought him he'd lift her up and carry her on his shoulders, the way he carried gear in a foundry. Maybe he was missing his work, missing the fatigue of it, anyway, the heat and exhaustion. The good part of work was that it wore you out.

When he opened the door, she scrambled in, her skirt belling. He kicked his tires. He'd be letting her off now. Good. He threw his jacket into the back of the van. "Where can I drop you, Flora?"

She rubbed her lower lip with her thumb. "It doesn't matter."

"What doesn't matter?"

"Take me to the bus station and I'll go on back."

"What the hell?"

"Raker, I lied, too. When Margie mentioned you'd be driving to Cleveland, I said I was coming here. I'll go on back down home now and you can do whatever you want."

"I don't get it."

"Sometimes I have to get out of that house." Her voice rose and cracked like a kid's when it changes.

He headed toward the towers of smoke that snaked up from the flats. The sun was brighter now, flashed off the chrome, heated his face as if he'd been running. He hadn't thought Flora kept any surprises in her. She sat silently, her hands in her jumper pockets, her face uplifted gravely to the sun, sweat beaded in the crescents beneath her eyes.

He wished he could just pull over to the side of the road and sleep, belly down, the way he'd warmed himself on the ledges of the quarry. Had Flora swum there? He couldn't remember, but she must have; all the kids did. He'd spent long afternoons there in the summers, and often gone back after school when fall came. The limestone tasted of salt. After he'd roasted himself there were marks on his belly and chest from the fissures, like incisions barely healed. He'd pretended he was a molting snake. It came to him now that, in the way a snake outgrows its old skin, he'd expected someday to slip off his disappointments. What fools kids are.

Without thinking it through, when he reached the shoreway he turned away from the city and headed east.

She turned to him. "Raker?"

"Let's go find us some geese."

She smiled, seeming not as startled with his plan as he was.

"There's a pint in my glove compartment."

She opened it, felt out the bottle, unscrewed the cap, and handed it to him. The whiskey ran warm down his throat and he imagined his headache easing already. He inhaled, then swallowed again. "Have some." He handed it back.

She drank, her throat working.

Probably because of the whiskey, his chest felt as though he'd taken off a tight shirt, or as though he'd been holding his breath under water and had just come up into air.

They ate the sandwiches as he drove. It was noon when they reached the peninsula, Presque Isle. The full force of the autumn sun lit the lake into a dazzling surface which looked more solid than brass, like molten metal in the foundry — too bright to look at even through safety glasses. Flora's gaze followed the shoreline but he blinked until he could pull the van off the road into the parking lot. The concrete-block changing house was shuttered, picnic tables stored on their sides, the chains that leashed trash barrels hung empty and clanging in the wind that scattered the fine, white sand. When Flora climbed out of the van beside him, her hair stood up like a cockscomb.

He took her elbow to guide her through the loose, furrowed sand down to the firmer shore near the water, and this time she didn't argue. Over the rush of the wind he heard the commotion of the geese that fed in the sheltered marsh beyond the pine woods. The birds rested here after crossing Lake Erie from Canada; it was the first land they came to.

On the lee side of the peninsula, the wind slowed and the sun pulsed up from the sand. Flora paused to pull off her raincoat, and he tied his jacket around his waist, rolled up his sleeves. He picked up a duck feather from the beach to put in her hand. She traced the quill with her forefinger, spread and then smoothed the barbs.

"From a teal," he said. "It's sort of blue."

She slipped the feather into the buttonhole of her jumper strap. Floundering, she followed him down the beach toward the path into the woods.

"What else do you see?"

He stepped over sticks, beer cans, seed pods and husks, candy bar wrappers, condoms. "Sand."

Then they were past the picnic grounds and into the tall cypresses trailing lengths of light-brown bark. The slanting trees closed overhead; Flora's steps came along surer now behind him on the sandy trail. Then they cleared the woods and entered the knee-high grass around the marsh.

Here the air smelled of pitch, of rank water, of bird droppings. Small leaves the color of copper pennies floated among the marsh reeds. At the far side of the lake the geese had settled to feed. Every few moments one flew singly up, wings slapping first water and then air, then, carving a trail across the burnished surface, settled back onto the brown water.

"There's about fifty. Canadian geese, the big ones," he whispered.

"I can hear them."

"When they take off near sunset it'll sound like a freight train."

He took her hand again to lead her to a broken picnic table kids must have dragged here. Pulling it forward onto the sand bank, he leveled the top. He showed her where to sit, facing the sun and the feeding geese. Then he folded his jacket for a pillow and lay down beside her on his back, his hands on his chest.

"I'm going to sleep for a while," he told her, though he guessed that was obvious.

When he closed his eyes he felt his body lengthen onto the planks of the table. Like a heavy hand on his head, the sun pressed him against the warm wood. His legs jerked, then his arms. He felt his jaw go slack and it seemed the table drifted heavily off the sand bar onto the surface of the weed-smelling marsh. He floated unmoored across the water in the bright path the sun laid down.

He woke to the heart-stopping tumult of the geese taking wing. The flock was already almost half in the air before their roar penetrated his dream. Their great, bent-bow wings lofted them into the red sky where they fanned out, at first randomly, then quickly forming their V toward the southern horizon. Excited, Raker sat up. A few stragglers soared last, wings clattering like branches in a wind storm. The din echoed across the pines and then the marsh was empty.

Until then he hadn't realized that Flora was gone. His mouth dry, his head aching, he scrubbed at his eyes, looked around him in the fading, ruddy light. Under his hands the table still held warmth; her raincoat lay where she'd been sitting.

Pulling on his jacket, he climbed up on the table. The marsh looked more like prairie than water, the surface as solidly green as hickory nut husks. A shiver of air moved the pine branches overhead and the tree frogs were starting up.

Bold as she was, she couldn't have gone far. The trail through the woods was winding. Even following right behind him, she'd stumbled. If she'd fallen into the water she'd have yelled, thrashed, called for help. He'd have wakened, wouldn't he?

Then he spotted her. She stood by a drowned scrub oak about a hundred feet along the shore, her profile to him. Ankle deep in the water, she dangled a shoe from each hand. Her face was raised to the sky where the geese had disappeared. Like a dancer, she lifted her body as though with a step she might ascend, too, and follow them, as though the impulse for their journey had been hidden in her and she'd only just now discovered the flight she had to take.

"Flora!"

She didn't answer. Rolling up his khakis, he pulled off his shoes, stuffed his socks into his pockets, and splashed out through the shallow, tepid water to her. When he touched her shoulder, carefully, the way he wakened his children from sleep, she started.

"Have they all gone?"

He turned her with his hand on her waist. She stumbled in the silky mud and he steadied her with his arm around her shoulders.

She looked back over her shoulder to the horizon. "Isn't there even one left?"

At the picnic table, she wiped her feet, pulled back on her knee socks, while he cleaned himself with his handkerchief. "There'll be more geese," he said more to himself than to her.

Then she reached for his arm, miscalculated the distance—though they sat side by side, shoulders touching—grabbed his knee, instead, but hung on. She swayed slightly as though she might topple from the bench. "Raker?" She whispered, then waited until he bent closer to hear. "I've *hated* my life."

He started to say something, he wasn't sure what, when she raised her hand to cover his mouth.

"Just let me say that. That's all."

"Flora, don't —"

"I'd like some of your whiskey, Raker." She got to her feet and started ahead of him toward the woods.

"What we need is some dinner." As he said it he knew it was true. They were exhausted and hungry, that was all.

He took her hand before she'd turned the wrong way and she hung on this time, like a child seeking comfort.

Although the sun had set, the maples made their own light like yellow lanterns. Maybe because he knew she couldn't see, or maybe because of this fine-grained, sepia light, the colors were especially vivid to him. Sumacs blazed like a string of bonfires along the edge of the woods. When they crossed the dunes beyond them, he saw bittersweet hanging in the pale grass like drops of blood.

She pulled the feather from her buttonhole and stroked it against her cheek, softened and girlish in the forgiving light. "What happens now, Raker?"

"First a little booze, then I buy you some dinner."

"That's not what I mean."

He knew that. Their footsteps whispered on the pine needles and then they were back on the beach. Balancing on the wind, as on a tightrope, a gull poised above the blue van, which tilted forward like a child's toy that had washed up with the bleached and twisted logs.

He took her to a rib place he remembered in Erie. A good choice — she could eat with her hands. They had barbecued ribs and fries and several beers. She ate eagerly and he dug in, too, hungrier than he'd remembered being in a long time. The beers relaxed her, and, smiling, she sucked the spicy sauce from her fingers. Country-and-western tunes played on the jukebox.

After the meal he was tired again. He wished he could drive back to the shore on Presque Isle, and listen to the lake lull him to sleep. He said, "You go wash up. We've got to be starting home."

Her face tensed. "If you go back tonight, you'll have to tell her."

"I know. It's time." He didn't know when he'd decided, but he didn't question it.

In the silence between them, the music seemed to come up louder. It would be midnight by the time he got home. As she always did, Margie would waken when he came to bed. That was as good a time as any to talk — the covers pulled up to their chins, the kids asleep, the house snug against the cold.

Lights from the jukebox played over Flora's face like the gleam from shallow water. He leaned forward to hear what she was saying to him. "—that we can come up to the lake again, Raker?"

He tried to compose an answer.

"Straight talk," she warned him.

"The season's almost over."

"That means *no*."

"I guess." He reached to rub a trace of sauce from her chin. "It was a good day."

"Yes."

"I'll remember it."

"Yes."

She stood up before he could, and, guiding herself by touch through the tables and chairs, made her way to the door. As she opened it, a gust of wind pulled it outward and wrapped her skirt against her legs. Like a swimmer lifting her head above the surface, she stepped forward into the darkness.

In High Country

"Unspoiled." Bill's dad spread the map out on the dining room floor, moving his coffee mug to lay it out flat. His heavy hands with fine, dark fur sprouting down from his wrists smoothed the folds. "Virgin territory, these mountains."

Bill felt like laughing and crying at the same time. It was a comedy: two city slickers from the North Shore enter virgin territory. But against his will he felt some excitement. Delivering groceries for the last grocery in Wilmette that took phone orders didn't seem like much of a summer, even if he had finally got his driver's license. "*We're* going to camp in virgin territory?"

"Why not? Why the hell not? We can learn. Never too old to learn." He bent over the map, traced the ridge line of the range. "The watershed," he announced, as though he'd discovered it on foot.

His dad's face seemed another kind of map to Bill: dark prints traced beneath his eyes, skin tight over his cheekbones, his chin shadowed by his evening beard, lips thinned by fatigue. Bill prodded an edge of the terrain map with his thumb. It crackled, some kind of waterproof paper — the real thing. "I don't see how we can, that's all."

His dad laid both hands down on the map, fingers outspread. He'd taken off his wedding band and that finger was pale, seemed swollen. He leaned forward, his heavy head wagging as he spoke. "So what's to stop us? What?"

Bill looked away. They hadn't talked about the divorce.

He saw his mom twice a week when she picked him up after track practice and took him out for supper at Scottie's. Even though he thought he shouldn't show too much interest, he always ran when he saw her pull up in her VW, the late sun catching her auburn hair. Since she'd left she seemed as mysterious and as remote as the high country his dad described; each time he saw her now he examined her for changes. When he jumped into her car she touched his arm, shyly. "Hey, old Billy," she said.

At Scottie's she drew her finger down the list of sandwiches as though she might choose something other than tuna on rye; she was on a diet now, that was new. He always ordered double cheese-burgers, and a chocolate shake. He was hungry, but mostly he knew it pleased her to see him eat.

Their talk was the same. "How's school? Track going okay, sweetie?" she'd ask, dipping her tea bag into her cup, her gray eyes watching him as he ate.

He'd stayed with his dad because he hadn't wanted to change schools now, his junior year. At least that's why he thought he'd stayed. He also thought maybe she'd come back. She'd sublet a tiny apartment in Winnetka; it didn't look permanent to him. "Track's fine."

She leaned toward him, holding her cup in both hands as though she were warming herself. "Are your shin splints better?"

"Some. Everybody's got them. How's business, Mom?"

She sold real estate. Usually she described recent customers to him, making the encounters into dramatic episodes. On the way to a movie one night, peering out of the back seat of a car filled with guys, he'd caught a glimpse of her in a pale dress going into Henrici's with a tall man, her arm laced through his. Could he have bought a house from her? Bill didn't want to ask. There was a lot it was better not to know. He stuck to school and business for conversation, and he hadn't told her that Dad was talking about backpacking, although he suspected his dad wanted him to. Frankly, he hadn't believed it would ever happen; his dad wasn't one to take risks.

But apparently they were going. The evidence was all around him. Besides the trail maps, his dad had bought tarps, insulated socks, fold-up plates with knives and forks that snapped on. The confu-sion of objects made Bill's head ache. It was too much. "Listen, Dad, what do you say I fix us some supper and we work on this after?"

His dad sat back on his haunches, his hands on his knees. "Yeah.
I've got to slow down. You can't master a map in an hour. And I
want to understand it. Not just learn what to do, but why. Do you
see what I mean?" He looked up at Bill from under his unruly eyebrows.

"You want to get it right?"

"That's it!" He slapped his thigh, then rose, brushing dust off his
knees; neither of them had talked about housekeeping yet. "I want
to get a grip on this whole thing."

The interstate was crowded with trucks and Bill wished they had
a CB; he and his dad didn't talk much. When Bill drove his dad either
studied his maps, lists, and manuals, or dozed, his thick legs splayed
out, one stockinged foot resting on the other. He wore his hiking
boots, breaking them in, he said. But when he napped he pulled them
off and they sat by his feet, lined up, the waxed laces as crisp as
fencing wire. Bill's boots were still in the box. They were stiff and
awkward; his feet felt trapped.

When his dad drove Bill let his forehead rest against the cool
window, his eyes slit almost shut against the June sun, a bronze
shadow on the glass: he had his mom's hair. The plains opened away
around them, rectangles of green or black patchworking all the way
to the horizon on every side. Mostly he watched the sky. Once he
saw a storm pass, far away and silently. Finally the first line of mountains appeared like a weather front moving in, a line of blue that
gradually became the plummy color of a bruise.

"The Rockies," his dad said. So he'd been watching, too. "We'll
make Denver tonight and cross the divide tomorrow. From there
we go up into high country."

Bill nodded. Until he'd seen the mountains he'd thought only of
what he was leaving behind; now they were on their way.

What surprised him most about the mountains was the quality of
light, air so clear that details far away were magnified. Sun dazzled
off the granite at the road edge and boulders seemed lit from within,
like street lights.

When his dad pulled the station wagon over to cool it down, Bill
walked to the guard rail for a better look. Cliffs rose sharply above

them and fell away below. He wondered if his mom had ever been to the mountains. She could barely force herself to walk along the bluff over Lake Michigan. He'd asked her once if she was afraid of heights. "I'm scared I might throw myself right over the edge. Maybe that's the same," she whispered. He pressed his knees against the guard rail and leaned out into the wind, the clean, pitchy gusts rising through the pines, rinsing over him like chill water. His chest was tight with excitement: *mountains*. Had his dad guessed *this*? He was in the car studying his map.

The town his dad had picked to start up from, Telluride, wasn't much—a trash of abandoned shacks left from gold rush times, small gray houses separated by empty lots scattered between them like gaps in a kid's teeth. Behind some of them aproned women worked in their kitchen gardens, early lettuce coming up, bean poles set in. Outside the hotel a tethered cow mooed in the early evening, waiting to be milked. It was like a foreign country.

They got their supper at the diner next to the hotel: pork chops and applesauce, a crater of gravy centered in the mashed potatoes. Bill ordered two glasses of milk. "The condemned men eat a hearty meal," he said.

"Hey," his dad said. "So far it's been all right. Something we've never done before. Admit that much."

"I admit that." He passed the plate of bread. "Do we get a guide here?"

"Guide? Why do you think I've been memorizing the maps? Some things you've got to do on your own, Billy. There comes a time in a man's life when he's got to take hold and *do* it, not think about it any more. Do *something*." He wiped up his gravy with a piece of bread, drawing circles on the white plate. "Are you game to try?"

"I'm here, aren't I?" It was the best he could do.

"I found a guy with a jeep who'll take us to the top of the range. We can hike down along the south slopes. Three nights of camping should do for a start."

Bill pushed his hair out of his eyes with the back of his hand. "Listen, Dad, would you call me Bill instead of Billy? In front of the guy with the jeep and all."

His dad nodded sternly. "Right, Bill." He nodded again to confirm the agreement, then signaled to the waitress for more coffee.

But in the morning nothing went as smoothly as Bill had expected from all the planning. By the time they got the packs loaded, his was so heavy he had to lean against the wall. His dad grunted, shouldering his, and slipped it off. "We've got to cut them by half. I didn't figure the altitude."

They repacked. The pickaxe went, half the food. They kept the sterno, left the stove. Tent, sleeping bags stayed, but no extra clothing. They took the snake bite kit, left the paperback books. When they finished the second time Bill's pack weighed in at thirty-five pounds on the "Your Weight and Your Fortune" scales in the hotel lobby. His fortune card read, "Your social life will improve."

His dad's pack weighed forty-four pounds. "That's the best we can do," he said, handing the fortune card to Bill. "Don't tell me if it's bad news."

"It says, 'Rethink your investment plans.' "

His dad shook his head. He was wearing his old army fatigue hat and army jacket with his name on the pocket: Hoornstra. "I don't want to think about anything for a while. Let's get out of here."

They stored their extra gear in the car, locked it, and by the time they met the jeep driver at the gas station it was almost noon.

The jeep road led upward through pine woods, then through open fields to a mining village, the buildings caved in, a graveyard with wooden markers tumbled down like broken fence posts. The treeline ended at the edge of the village and the switchbacks on the narrow road were sharper. The jeep driver had to back up to make the turns. Finally he backed and hauled around the last switchback and pulled up on the highest rise, a ridge about fifteen feet across. A faintly marked trail led away to the south like a stripe down a cat's spine, the mountain yellow and tawny with streaks of iron. Scattering rock chips, the jeep pulled away. The driver waved, "Luck, fellas!"

They were alone. They had a quick snack of peanut butter and crackers while his dad gave the map a final look. On all sides the mountain fell away from them. Scrub pine and piñon were gray shadows in the upland valleys far below. The insect sounds that had scoured the noon fields they had come through were gone. There was only the wind. Bill studied the narrow trail. His mom would faint if she could see that stone face sheared away on both sides, he thought. He focused on the height, trying to form an idea of what such space might mean to her. She would leap, she couldn't help herself: she would be killed. He imagined his mother plummeting through the drafts where a hawk hung below them, sailing in and out of the shadows. For the first time he thought of her not as just his mom, but as a person with deep fears, and he was afraid for her. "I bet women don't hike up here," he blurted, but his dad had the map spread out on a slab of rock and didn't answer.

Hiking was harder than Bill had guessed. Within half an hour his heels began to ache and sting. He should have broken his boots in; he knew better. His pack slipped until he got the straps right, and then he felt as though he were carrying a boulder. His dad led the way, shoulders hunched, feet sliding on loose rock. After less than an hour he stopped, slipped off his pack, laid himself spread-eagle beside the trail.

Bill lay down beside him, gasping. "Slow down?"

"Right." His voice was hard to hear in the wind.

When they started again they went very slowly and by the time they stopped to set up their tent they were still far above the highest timber. The last sun was no warmer than light glancing off ice. Around them tiny tundra blooms were confetti specks of orange and red, the rocks coated with lichen.

Bill ate what his dad spooned onto his tin dish — something that tasted of tomato paste. They had some chocolate, and after they wiped off their plates they had cocoa. There wasn't much to say, but he and his dad had never talked much. It was dark by 8:30 and they crawled into their sleeping bags, feet pointing downhill.

"Any bears up here?" Bill asked.

"The ranger said not."

"When did you talk to a ranger?"

"At the gas station. You were in the can. He lives in one of these upland valleys. Says there's a lot of deer and elk poaching around here. But no bears."

His dad's breath smelled of chocolate. Only a moment had gone by before Bill heard him snore. He closed his eyes, feeling an edge of stone against his ribs. The wind howled in their tent and he imagined wolves. It wouldn't be good to think about home, he knew that. Then he felt himself hurtling backwards into sleep as though he were falling from the side of the gorge into the space wind had hollowed out below him.

When he woke in the morning it was hard to move. He watched from his sleeping bag as his dad crept around their camp site, piling bits of dried moss onto the fire. His thick, gray hair was matted; he'd been in the same position each time Bill woke during the night — knees drawn up, face buried inside his bag.

Around them the mountains loomed dense and metallic. "Christ!" Bill whispered.

"Hey," his dad said.

"You know what I mean." Bill raised his arm to trace the horizon line of sharp-edged peaks.

"It's a lot," his dad said: his gift.

That day was better. They paced themselves, urging each other to stop, to rest. They had a snack of nuts or dried fruit every hour or so. Bill took off his windbreaker and tied it to his pack, and by the time they reached the first fork in the trail his dad's sides were dark with sweat. A stream ran beside the new trail. The rushing water smelled of clean stones, of rain, and small trout leaped next to the bank. Bill swung along behind his dad, whistling. Maybe they would become outdoorsmen, after all. Who knew what was possible?

That night they camped in a meadow by the stream. There was soft grass under their tent and the wind had died down. His dad fixed beef and noodles. After, they built the fire up and sang a few songs, mostly ones that Bill remembered from Y camp. He hugged his knees, feeling the fire on his face like a comforting hand. An owl circled low over the meadow; after mice, Bill guessed. The moon had come up and it gazed down like a white eye. At home he had never paid much attention to the moon.

But in his sleeping bag, Bill was restless. "You know any stories?" His dad grunted no.

"I wish I had a book."

"Too heavy." He was falling asleep, his voice deepening.

"I just want something to do. It's only nine."

"Long day, Bill." There was an emphasis on the single syllable of his name; his dad was keeping his word.

"I know."

"So go on to sleep."

"Mind if I sing some more?"

No answer.

So he sang. He started in on "Rock and roll is here to stay," moved on to "Blueberry Hill," then went way back in time for "One little, two little, three little Indians."

"That's the first song Mom taught me," he said, not especially talking to his dad.

Silence.

Then from inside his sleeping bag his dad said, "Wrong. 'Baby's bed is like a boat,' that was her song for you."

"I forget that one."

Startled, he heard his father's voice start up, low and muzzy with fatigue.

> Baby's bed is like a boat,
> Sailing out to sea.
> When morning comes then baby's boat
> Comes sailing back to me.

After the first verse there was silence again.

Bill turned on his side, curling himself around his jacket. He felt a painful but not unwelcome ache of consciousness: after all, he loved his dad, no matter that he was clumsy or misjudged what he could do, no matter even that somehow he'd let Mom leave, hadn't been able to stop her, persuade her, love her enough, whatever it was he couldn't do or couldn't be. "We've hiked a long way up here," he said by way of thank you, but his dad was asleep.

In the morning they followed the trail through the high meadow grass, birds flying up around them. After lunch the pines and aspen closed over the trail and the light was dappled; if there were deer moving Bill couldn't see them. At the side of the stream the trail forked. "Which way?" Bill called back. He was leading.

His dad slipped off his pack and pulled the map from his hip pocket, opened it, rubbed his two-day beard with his knuckles while he studied it. "This doesn't show any fork here."

Bill chucked a stone into the stream. The trail beside the water was rocky but looked more direct than the one that crossed over and into the woods again. "So what do we do?"

His dad looked up, brow furrowed, eyebrows almost meeting. "Don't know."

"Is there a wrong choice?"

His dad looked down at the map again as if the answer to Bill's question might be there. "Don't know that, either."

Bill shifted his weight, impatient. "We got a lot to learn."

His dad pulled on his pack but didn't answer. Overhead birds settled back into the pines. The stream sounded like leaves rustling.

"Well?"

His dad was looking down into the stream; he looked up, startled, and shrugged. Moving ahead of Bill he started down the trail beside the stream.

After the first quarter mile the trail grew suddenly steeper. He motioned Bill to go ahead of him. "Something's wrong," he said as Bill inched past.

"We'll get down quicker, that's all." But he was anxious: he had to concentrate on each step, set his feet in sideways, grasp at saplings where the stones were slick and wet underfoot. It was like climbing down a broken ladder and no end in sight. They climbed like that an hour, two. "Want to rest?" His heart crashed with fatigue; no matter how he dug in at each step the rocks slid from beneath his boots.

"A little farther. Let's get the hell out of here."

So Bill pushed on, tasting the sweat that ran onto his lips. When his dad fell Bill heard, rather than saw, the fall—the wild scattering of rocks, birds beating up, the thud of a man's body careening into stones as he slid. The cry was Bill's, "No!"

He ripped off his pack and half stumbled, half climbed back up the steep trail. His dad lay on his side, his head on the trail, legs in the stream, his pack torn open and foil packets and cookware scattered around him. His face was as gray as the stones that pillowed him. "My goddamn knee," he moaned as Bill crouched by him. "Oh, god! My knee!"

Bill felt as though all his blood had suddenly been forced into the valves of his heart. It was like the stories he'd read of parents lifting cars off their children: he could pick up his father and carry him on his back as easily as he could his pack. "I'll take you!"

"Just get me out of the water." He held up his arms to Bill.

When Bill bent to pull, his feet slipping in the stream, his strength left him as quickly as it had come. His dad's foot was wedged. When he tugged to pull him free his dad screamed, a long scream that grew in size and weight and then dropped off sharply. The trail darkened as though the afternoon light had been drained away by the cry. Bill closed his eyes a moment and when he opened them he could see again. Lifting more than pulling, he got his dad up on the trail.

"How far to the ranger, Dad?"

"Cut me a staff."

"I can go!"

"Do what I say."

Bill cut a pine branch the length of a ski pole. Clumsy, he worked too fast, chose a crooked one, but his dad seized it. Leaning on the staff and Bill's shoulder, his father crept back onto the trail. They didn't speak. His father's lips were white, his jaw clenched as though holding back another scream. Bill glanced back once at the abandoned backpack, his dad's sleeping bag unfurled into the stream like the body of a drowned man.

Within an hour—or was it more, time was measured by their halting steps—the trail they followed abruptly joined a fire road. They'd been beside a road all this time; for all their climbing they'd never been far away at all.

"Wait here, Dad. I can go faster alone."

This time his dad didn't argue. Cradling his knee in his hands, he sank down in the dry grass between the ruts of the fire road. "Hurry," he said without moving his lips, the word an exhalation. Bill began to run.

By dusk he spotted a thin line of smoke: the ranger's cabin. The ranger had a jeep. The headlights splashed over the fire road as though over rough water. In a couple of hours they had his dad in to see the doctor. Nothing broken; bruises, a sprain. The doctor gave Bill's dad an envelope of pills for the pain. "Don't worry," he said.

"Nothing serious." He'd turned from them before they reached his office door.

"I'll put you up with me for the night." The ranger was tanned already and wore a red ski cap pushed jauntily over one ear.

"Caused you enough trouble," his dad said.

"It's my job." He stroked his yellow moustache. "But I'd sure like company."

His dad turned his hands palms up, asking Bill to decide.

"Thanks. That would be great." Bill's voice was too loud in the small waiting room.

"I'd like a drink," his dad said. He didn't look up.

"You got it," the ranger said.

At the ranger's cabin the whiskey bottle was already out on the counter beside the dish detergent. The ranger rinsed a jelly glass, poured some whiskey straight up and handed it to Bill's dad at the table where he sat, foot propped up on an extra chair. "Take it easy, with those pills. I'll fix chow."

Bill brought in his pack, took off his boots, then his dad's, set them by the door to clean in the morning. He laid out forks and knives, paper napkins. The delicious, dizzying aroma of onions and potatoes frying in bacon drippings made his stomach moan with hunger. The ranger poured a beer for himself and a glass of milk for Bill. They ate without talking, his dad working on the whiskey as well as the fried eggs, fried potatoes, slices of ham.

After supper Bill cleared the table and washed up. Behind him the two men talked. His dad had his hiking map spread out on the table, the crackle sounding like a fire. Bill went at the dishes slowly, the warm water making him lazy.

"You started on the right trail, no doubt about that. See, there? You started off just right." After each sentence the ranger paused to suck on his pipe.

"And this fork?"

"Right there, too."

"I studied it." His dad's voice blurred with the pain medicine and the whiskey. "I studied so hard."

"You were going right."

"But somewhere things went wrong."

"Let's have another look."

Bill glanced back to see the ranger, still in his ski hat, bent over the map, head close to his dad's. "You were doing fine here at the meadows."

His dad shook his head. "It's different. I mean, on a map it's all so clear. When you're *in* it things aren't the same. You don't know until it's too late."

The ranger turned the map toward him, then back again. He tapped the stem of his pipe against his teeth. "The fact is you got onto the goat path. You weren't on any hiking trail at all. You must have seen that," he said gently.

It was hard for Bill to hear his dad. "I thought maybe that's how hiking trails were."

The ranger slapped the table with his open hand. "But how the hell would you know? I mean, you hadn't done it before! You were trying something new."

Bill put the last plate in the drainer and took the coffee pot to the table. He poured an inch into his dad's cup, although it was still almost full. The ranger held his empty cup out for more.

His dad bent his head and rested it on his arms. "I got it wrong, it's just that simple. Dead wrong."

"Hey, man, what did you lose? You're here. You ain't hurt bad."

The ranger thought his dad was still talking about camping.

"Nothing's broke that can't be fixed or bought new!" The ranger rocked back in his chair and laughed, winking at Bill.

There were two wooden bunks in the spare room. The lantern lit the rough pine walls, the calendar with a picture of a girl smiling over a basket of apples, her breasts full at the basket rim. There were no curtains. The moon rose high above the pines, outdistancing the branches, its light a second lantern in the dim room.

Bill helped his dad unbutton his flannel shirt, ease his trousers over his bruised knee. There were a couple of inches of whiskey in the tumbler, and his dad set it close to the bunk on the floor where he could reach it.

Bill turned down the lantern wick and climbed into the upper bunk.

The pillow prickled and smelled of mold. His bunk was on a level with the upper window and a square of moonlight lay on his blanket.

From below his dad asked, "Want to sing?"

"No, Dad. Go on to sleep."

"I feel like singing."

"Dad, you're kind of smashed. Get some sleep."

"My goddamn leg hurts."

Bill climbed down and put his pillow under his dad's knee to take the pressure off. "Better?"

"Better." He didn't open his eyes.

Bill bundled his jacket into a pillow, smelling of pine and smoke. "Night, Dad."

There was silence for a while, and then his dad began to sing — a broken, atonal line. "Five foot two, eyes of blue, and oh what those blue eyes can do . . ." His voice trailed off.

Bill drew his knees up to his chest. His longing for home left him as alert as if he'd just awakened. He was sure he would not sleep at all, he would watch the moon until it set, wishing for home the way it used to be, his mother there.

Long after Bill thought he must have fallen asleep, his dad whispered up to him. "Billy? Awake?"

"Yeah."

"Listen. I got to ask you something. A promise. Don't tell, okay? When you see her again, don't *tell.*"

There was the terrible sound of his father trying not to cry.

Bill turned his face against his jacket. His mouth was dry with panic, as though his dad's sorrow and shame had entered him like a fever and become his own. He clenched his teeth, biting down until his head ached with effort. When he heard his father's breathing steady into sleep he opened his eyes. The patch of moonlight had crept up to his chest like a cat and nestled there. Over the dark pines the owl circled in wide, descending spirals through the cloudless night.

The Courtship of the Thin Girl

Jerry phoned me. "Mike, come on over to our condo Sunday for some tennis. Meet my wife, Karen."

Karen got on the phone. "And dinner here, after, to get acquainted. Jer tells me you're his new wonder boy at Westside Clinic, and I want to meet you!"

After I accepted, she rambled on; she'd run into the daughter of an old friend and would like to invite her, too. The girl's name was Laura Hale, and her dad had done the insurance work for Jerry's clinic before he'd died of a heart attack a few months ago. Laura had just graduated from college and was back to take care of the family home and her younger sister—all by herself; her mom had passed away several years ago. It was a lot of work; Laura was very brave. What did I think of asking her to join us?

Of course I tried to sound pleased. What the hell could I do? Jerry was the best orthopod on the North Shore; I wanted to get off to a good start with my first job. But I pictured the brave Laura Hale like a woman from a Victorian novel: small, shy, and yet determined, with glasses.

After tennis with Jerry, I took my turn in their shower and when I came out, damp in my clean khakis, a slim blonde I guessed must be Laura was setting the table on the deck. She wore a black sundress that showed off her tan, and her hair was loose, thick and in motion as she bent forward to lay knives across the table. Her hair parted, falling along her shoulders, and I could see the raised bones of her spine, each one as discrete as a pearl. She turned to smile at me as if she'd known I was watching.

"You two look like brother and sister," Karen said. "All that light hair, those brown eyes. You're a matched set."

"Fine by me," Laura said. "I'll take that."

I just grinned.

Jer said, "Mike, here, takes anything he can get." He roughed his wife's curly hair as though she were his dog. She pretended to strangle him with the heavy gold chain he wore.

We had good steaks and an indifferent salad of iceberg lettuce. Laura brought iced brownies to go with the fresh peaches and, at her urging, I ate three, picking up the crumbs with the tips of my fingers while Karen rattled on about life in the condos. When Laura described her days — tennis lessons, the gym, real estate classes, sailing — I decided she'd get along just fine running the old family manse or whatever and raising her kid sister. I guessed she knew lots of people and got out as much as she wanted to; Karen didn't need to do her any favors. But then there was the other thing.

My medical training had taught me to recognize that she'd been anorexic. I put her illness in the past tense because she was thin, but not what I'd call emaciated. Slim. Still, there was that cast to her skin like a green underpainting beneath her tan, a hollowness above her eyes. Her hands and feet seemed slightly too large for her. I spotted her nipples through the sheer sundress but she had no breasts, and her hips were narrow as a boy's. The boyishness of her figure contrasted with the beauty of her face, full lips turned down slightly, straight eyebrows, narrow nose, that tawny hair.

I felt a tenderness for her. It was the tenderness a parent might feel for an injured child, even though the child is not his own. Although she seemed so confident, at one time she'd damaged herself and the marks were still on her.

When I thought about it later, I realized that from the very first I was hooked on the certifiably insane idea that I could care for her, nurse and cajole and nourish the woman out of the boyish girl. It was an automatic response: I wanted to save her.

"You kids talk while we clean up," Jerry said.

While he and Karen cleared the table and made coffee, I asked Laura, "Can I take you home? I've got my car."

"You can take me anywhere," she smiled. "Whoever you are."

"Well, it's *me*." I smiled down at the brownie crumbs I was chasing, feeling as though I'd said something profound.

But the rest of the evening went differently than I'd expected. I'd hoped to take her to a bar, have a couple of beers, hear her story — maybe tell her mine, such as it was. But she wanted to go home. "Karen told you about my sister, didn't she?"

She had.

"Di's home alone. She's been real upset about going to bed since I let the housekeeper go. She's never had a sitter. I told her I'd be home by her bedtime." Then she added, "I'd like to see what it's like to have you at the house, okay?"

I was disappointed, but didn't say so. It was a typical Chicago May night, warm and humid, a faint, chemical smell almost like cinnamon in the air from the factories. We rolled the windows all the way down and she put her arm out, like I did — "holding down the roof," we'd called it when I was in high school. I felt almost as though I was in high school again, thrown off my guard by Laura and her domestic necessities, waiting to see which way she'd move.

I pulled up in front of her house, a narrow stucco two-story under oaks so thick they blocked the streetlights from the front walk. Lights were on in the downstairs rooms and a mosquito candle flickered on the porch. "It's my place, now," she said.

She directed me to pull around the block and park in her drive-way on the lane; the police ticketed cars without town stickers this close to the park. "Let me have a peek at Di and then let's walk along the bluff. I want to show you Lake Michigan from up here." She jumped out and ran ahead.

I parked behind the Chevy that was in the drive and walked back around the corner to her front porch. She stood on the front steps, waiting for me. "I thought you'd run away." She took my hand and turned toward the park, beyond which I could see the opaque dark-ness that would be the lake. "Don't let's talk now, Mike. Let's just *be*. This is my favorite place in the world."

So I followed her, enjoying the light, tensed grip of her hand in mine. Her bones were narrow, like glass straws. I could easily lift her; her weight would be nothing to me. From time to time she smiled and pointed: a raccoon, an owl circling over the park, visible now and then through the trees, a cat hunting in the long grass near the edge of the bluff.

Away from the streetlights the night closed in around us. In the park the trees roofed us over, but at the edge of the bluff where she led me the whole sky appeared suddenly, vast and milky, a sheen of stars seen faintly through the haze. I gasped when she wrapped her free arm around a precariously rooted oak and leaned out to point to the beach below. The sand was lighter than the water. Down the beach two fires burned, tiny figures moving around them. I held her hand more tightly when she swung back to me. She stood quite still beside me and slowly I heard the sounds of the lake, sighing like the wind off the plains. The lake smell made me think of rust or salt. Far out from shore, lights of freighters moved south toward the ports of Chicago and Gary.

"Do you want to climb down the bluff with me?" she whispered. "I can do it with my eyes closed."

"Next time." I realized as I answered that I'd made a commitment.

We turned to cross the park back to her house and I slipped my arm around her waist, not pulling her close, but just to feel her there. The distances of the night made me sad. In med school I'd grown used to being alone; maybe she'd ask me in and we could talk.

At her porch she went ahead of me. "Di? Me again." A moth beat at the screen, flying out when the screened door swung wide. In spite of the mosquito candle, I heard a high whine by my ear and slapped. My hand came away from my forehead damp. It was hotter than I'd realized. Her hand had been cool in mine.

In the long front room a small girl sat in the middle of a Persian rug, a box of crayons spread out around her. She looked up when I followed Laura in. Her solemn, round face, sunburned cheeks, and shoulders shone in the soft light. Her dark hair was in braids and she wore a pair of bib overalls cut off short, no shirt under.

"Di, this is Dr. Duffield." Laura paused by the couch. "Di got too much sun at the beach today."

"I forgot the zinc oxide," Di said, as though she and her sister had been over this point several times. "It was in the cupboard with the dog food but I couldn't find it." She picked tar off her bare foot.

"I'll put you to bed now." Instead of asking me to wait, Laura led me back to the front door. "It's a lot less trouble if you walk around the sidewalk to the garage. We've got a puppy in the back-yard and she'll wake up and remember we took her away from her mother and howl like she's done every night."

Behind me, Di said, "Her name's Daisy."

I found myself back at the porch door. "I'd like to see you again."

"I'd like that, too. A lot, actually. But not tomorrow. I have to think about you for a while."

Tomorrow? That startled me. I'd thought I might ask her to a movie and a hamburger after, maybe in a week or so. It was as if she had a plot outline I didn't have, or at least a different set of expec-tations.

"I'll be in touch." Over Laura's shoulder I saw Di appear in the lighted doorway, look out at me, one bare foot propped on the other.

"Was he your date?" Di asked, although I hadn't left yet.

"Yes and no," Laura said, smiling as she leaned toward me. It was the most intimate look she'd given me all evening. I wondered what the kid made of this glamorous young woman who liked to run things.

There was nothing left to do except to wave goodnight and make my way around the corner and back to my car. The sidewalk was tipped by roots and pieces had broken away. I watched my step. From the ravine behind the lane a whippoorwill's falling notes sounded.

I climbed in my Ford, rummaged for the keys I'd placed under the seat for safekeeping; how had I expected I might lose them from my pocket? Had I guessed I'd lie on the beach with her?

While I fumbled in the dark to find the right key, I sensed more than saw her run to my car from the back gate of her yard. The black of her dress blended with the fence and the hedge, but I caught the pale shape that was her face, a blur that was her bare arm. She darted in front of the car and was at my window, handing me some-thing. Her breath smelled of the fruit we'd eaten.

"You *will* call, won't you?" Her lips brushed my cheek and then she drew back. "That's my number." I realized I had a scrap of paper in my hand. "Don't lose it."

"Don't worry." She was already running back to the gate, had disappeared again. I waited a moment before I turned my lights on, keeping an image of her face. When my lights came on they lit a metal sign, Beware of the Dog, that had been nailed to the gate, waist high, as though the kid had been given the task and put it at her own height. A light went on upstairs in the house but no one looked out.

Back in my little apartment I was bored. I got myself a beer, pulled a kitchen chair onto the narrow balcony overlooking Route 41. Below, cars streamed by on their way out of the Sunset Drive-in, couples tucked behind the steering wheels as though both were driving. I propped my feet up on the railing and studied the lovers. Feeling randy.

Now that I wasn't with Laura, she seemed more eccentric than when we were together. Earlier, what we'd done was natural. Then she'd both sent me away and run after me — a mixed message. I wanted something more substantial. I decided she was making herself more mysterious than she was.

Then my impatience gave way to the other, stronger feeling: I wanted a woman. Flesh and blood. I didn't want mystery and intuition and responsibility for the family home and the kid. I wanted a normal woman, one who made it clear what she was about. One with tits. I crumpled my beer can. I felt like howling down to the cars passing below, "I want a woman!" like the lunatic in that Fellini film I'd seen who climbs a tree and refuses to come down until someone promises him he can screw a dame.

Then I tried to concentrate on the simple pleasure of walking in the park with Laura Hale. She was okay. In a few days I'd call her. I'd see what would happen.

Just before morning, the phone woke me. The hospital, I thought, but I wasn't on call. An emergency, then. I tried to sound alert, though I was groggy, coming out of sleep. "Dr. Duffield here."

She laughed. "Jerry is really mad! I woke him up to get your phone number."

"Laura?"

"Of course. Do lots of women call you at five in the morning?" I pushed to my elbow. "What's up?"

"I have something to tell you."

"Now?"

"Now is when it's happening."

"When what's happening?" Was she playing a game?

"My period."

"Your period," I repeated, the doctor reassuring a patient by following a list of symptoms. The truth was I had trouble understanding her; maybe she was on drugs.

"You don't know what that means?"

"You're menstruating." Checking my diagnosis. Why would she call me at five in the morning to tell me she was menstruating? Last night she hadn't even wanted me to stay and talk.

"Yes!" she cried, as though I'd understood something complicated.

What should I say now? Before I could decide, she rushed on, "Isn't that amazing?"

I sat up, pushed my pillow behind my back and settled in to try to help her make sense. "Is 'amazing' good or bad?"

"Mostly it's just amazing. I've never had a period before. This is my first. I've gained a lot of weight these last months and I kept hoping. My doctor was hopeful, too. Then I met you last night and when I woke up a little while ago I knew. I absolutely knew, and I was right. Don't you see, Mike? It's some kind of sign."

I remembered what I'd read about anorexia, the medical reports. A starving woman loses her fertility quickly, the frantic attempt of the organism to save itself; those studies from the concentration camps provided invaluable data. In a young girl, the most common victims of anorexia, delayed adolescence. What else? "You never had a period at all?"

"Never. It's all so complicated, Mike. The important thing is that although I was sick, now I'm better. I'm well. This proves it. I'm normal, don't you see?"

I thought I did. "So you called me?"

"I had to share this with someone. With you, I guess. It seems connected some way with meeting you, although I know it must be coincidence."

"Yes."

"You're angry I woke you?"

"I'm glad you shared it with me." That seemed safe.

She seemed not to hear the professional tone, or my reservations. "Oh, Mike!"

"Do you want to talk about it some more?" I asked tentatively, wondering if I did.

"Not now. Soon. I'm too excited now."

"Do you want me to call you?" Wondering if I wanted to call.

"Yes. Call me. I knew you'd understand. I trust you. You'll call me." And she hung up.

I lay staring at the window, the green hazing into pink as the sun came up through the exhaust fumes and mist. My room was small and unfamiliar in the faint light, as though I'd gone to sleep in one room and wakened in another. Karen had told me that Laura Hale was twenty-one.

I was very tired, but I couldn't go back to sleep. After a while I got up and fried myself some eggs. She trusted me; what was I going to do about that?

I waited three days before I called. I phoned from my new office in Jerry's clinic. I didn't have time to talk, I said, but I'd like to take her out for a bite to eat soon. Tonight? No, I had a conflict. I chose a time a few days off; I wanted to stay in control of things.

We went out for hamburgers and beers. This time it was as I'd hoped it would be. Sitting in a booth in the Irish Waters, we talked long and quietly. We held hands now and then across the table as she spoke of her life, and I of mine. It was an intimate conversation, the kind I'd been hungry for. She told me her sad family stories. "Things are going better for you," I assured her.

"You've been through tough times, too," she said. "I can tell. It's made you sympathetic. You're such a good man."

I wanted to believe I was.

"Mike, I do trust you. I trust you absolutely."

Then we were in my car, parked out on a deserted lane overlooking the lake. The air was sweet with lilacs, an undertone of onion grass cutting through the perfume. Bob Dylan was singing "Lay, lady, lay, lay across my big brass bed," on the radio, and Laura's head was on my shoulder. She took my left hand, kissed the palm, and then slowly and deliberately licked and sucked each of my fingers. When I kissed her lips, they parted easily, and I felt her tongue there, too. I drew back and looked into her face, the pure oval, creamy skin. Her eyes were open. "You can't convince me you're not something special, Mike."

I didn't want to convince her. She was pulling my damp hand up under her skirt to press against her even damper panties. "Would you like my pussy?" she asked. As though this was the reward for my trustworthiness.

Yes, I would. Very much.

"Di's home tonight. She's going to sleep over at a friend's house tomorrow."

How about my place then?

"I want you in *my* bed."

I wanted to be there, too.

"So we have to wait until tomorrow. You don't mind?"

I minded. How about here in my car?

"We can do better than that. You understand, don't you?"

I wasn't sure.

"We should go back now. I have to put Di to bed."

In a daze I backed out of the lane, bushes slapping my face and arms as I leaned out the window to find the tracks. At her house she kissed me once more. "Promise?" she asked. "Tomorrow night?"

I promised.

But when we were alone the next night she was almost formal. She lit candles while I undressed and then she undressed in the bathroom. When we lay down together we were ceremonial, I thought — forehead to forehead, hands on each other's shoulders. I'd hoped she'd be wanton.

Later, we had iced tea and talked. Our conversation was more relaxed than our caresses had been. But she clung to me when I left. "I'm so glad!" she whispered.

I *thought* I was.

At 3:10 that morning she phoned me. I sat up in the dark, disbelieving the illuminated digits of my clock, disbelieving that she was doing this again. I tried to make out what she was saying. I imagined how her face was crumpled by her sobs, but her words didn't make sense. Her sobs seemed wrenched up out of her lungs like water from a woman who's almost drowned.

"Laura! For god's sake, are you sick?"

She said something, Sever? Lever?

I tried my doctor's voice. "Slow down. Tell me slowly."

That worked. At least I made out a few words. "You won't love me! You'll never love me! You'll feel sorry for me but you'll never love me. Never!"

Steadily, as though to a drunk, I said, "Try to calm down. I'm coming back. I'll be there in a few minutes."

I yanked on jeans, a shirt, and drove the twenty minutes down an almost deserted highway, a few trucks passing me in the dark tunnel of the night. Had she drunk too much, taken some drug? When I'd left she'd seemed fine, just fine.

She was waiting for me in the darkened front door. In the dim light her face was disfigured, as though she'd been tortured. She fell against me and pulled the door shut behind us.

She let me help her back up the stairs, let herself be eased onto the tangled sheets. "I don't know what's the matter! I need you so much!" She turned her face into the pillow and after a moment I took my clothes off and lay down beside her, touched her wet face.

"It's all right."

"It'll never be all right! *I* know and *you* don't."

"It's all right."

"I feel so awful! I don't know what's wrong!" She clung to my shoulders. She wore a sweatshirt and no panties. Her legs were chill when they touched mine. I drew the sheet over the two of us, wondering how this had come about in my life.

"I'm here." I stroked her shoulder.

"You'll never love me! I have no substance!" She faltered on that word and tried again. "Substance. I'm hollow inside." Then she buried her face against my chest and I felt her tears there. "You'll never love me."

I held her a long time, at first tightly, and then when her crying eased, more gently. "If I fall asleep, don't leave me," she begged.

I didn't leave her. In the growing light I searched out the shapes in her room that had been lit with the candles earlier. Her white skirt lay on her dresser, straw sandals sat on top of a lacquer box, her blouse was crumpled on a chair. The curtains moved in the light breeze that came in off the lake. Mostly I listened to the lake, its steady breath against the beach. It would be good to swim out into the lake in this pearly light, head toward the Michigan shore.

I tried to reconstruct the evening: we'd made love, I'd been gentle, maybe too gentle. "What would you like?" I asked, but she had asked for nothing at all. Like a married couple we'd washed separately, after, and gone downstairs to sit on the porch. She talked about her father; I talked about the clinic. What was there in any of that to bring her to hysteria? I hadn't told her that I loved her. Could I?

After a long while she said, "You have to go." She didn't open her eyes and I wasn't sure if she'd slept, or just pretended to.

"Okay."

Then she grasped my hand, the one she'd licked and sucked so suggestively only two nights before, and kissed the back of it as though she was my slave. "You're so good, Mike! You saved me tonight. I don't know what I might have done."

I drew myself out of her arms, and trying to keep down the edge of panic that pushed me faster, I pulled on my pants and shirt.

"You'll call this afternoon?" The sheet was down again, her hands crossed on her chest. The edge of her sweatshirt came just above her tuft of auburn hair. I pulled up the sheet, tucked her in.

"I'll try."

Then I let myself out of the house. I pulled away down the empty street, forcing myself to drive slowly. I drove to a donut shop and had two sugar donuts and coffee. If I went home, she might call again. What the hell was I going to do? What would happen now?

When I called her at five that afternoon she laughed about a tennis game she'd won, about Di's efforts to housebreak Daisy; she was trying a new chicken recipe and was cleaning cupboards. It was as though her weeping hadn't happened.

Except that it had.

"I don't have much appetite when there's just Di and me, and I'm trying to gain. Couldn't you join us? I made a terrific apple pie."

I hesitated.

"Please?"

My reluctance had forced the plea from her. She'd hated begging, I knew. Quickly, before my silence reduced her to pleading, I said, "Sure."

The apple pie was great, tart with cinnamon. I had two pieces and then helped Di do a crossword puzzle while Laura did the dishes. After, I taught them Five Card Draw and Spit in the Ocean, betting pennies.

After Di had been put to bed Laura asked me if we couldn't make love again. This time I handled her more roughly. She was so light, so pliant, I could easily turn her this way, that way. "Do you like this?" I whispered. "Or this?" But she didn't answer. Her silence had its own seductive power. I did as I wanted.

I must have slept for a while, for I started awake. She was tensed, her breath on my chest shallow and uneven. Against her forehead I asked, "Are you okay?"

"Yes."

"Sure?"

"Yes."

I thought her voice trembled and the wild crying of the night before came back to me. "Listen, Laura?"

"Yes."

"You've got to promise me something. It's important."

"Yes. Anything."

"No more crying. It's too hard on you. It's too hard on me. And there's nothing to cry about."

"No, I won't cry. I don't want to. It's too awful. I won't."

Later, when I unlatched the screened door I reminded her, "You won't cry. What if Di heard you? She'd be scared to death."

"Like *you* were."

Even in the dark I saw that she was smiling. She was taunting me. She was herself again; she was okay. We were okay. I could make everything all right. Although I didn't love her, I had a love *for* her. That would be enough. Wouldn't it?

In any case even then it was somehow too late. A choice had been made. We got married on Thanksgiving day.

Saturday Night in Pinedale, Wyoming

He looked in the side door of the Cowboy Bar and Grill, smoke thick, the juke loud, the air full of hamburger grease. A couple of the hands from the Lazy D called out to him, "Hey, Matt!" But he just waved at them. Most of the guys were half-crocked already and it was only 9:00 P.M. Better to be alone, he decided. He bought a pint of apricot brandy at the Liquor Drive-in, snugged it into his pocket. "Where you heading," Verna asked through the drive-in window, her little sausage curls bouncing. But he just winked. What the hell, so he was doing his laundry—no need to tell her that. No need to advertise.

He pulled his muddy pickup right up to the door of the coin laundry, the headlights beaming into the bright, empty room. The coin laundry smelled of soap and mold, the windows still steamed up from a busy afternoon. After the crisp October air outside, he found it hard to get his breath. He stuffed his jeans into one washer, his shirts, towels, long johns into another, poured in the little boxes of detergent he bought from the dispenser. Then he unsnapped the checked shirt he was wearing and dropped that in, too. He shoved his quarters into the coin tray and watched until the suds boiled up against the glass. He pulled a paper cup from the dispenser in the bathroom, dragged a chair over to the folding table and sat, propping his feet up to search through the coverless *Field and Stream*s for one he hadn't seen. The brandy was warm, smelled of ripe apricots. He held a mouthful on his tongue until he felt the burn through the sugar, then let it trickle down his throat. Not such a bad way to spend an hour, the warmth spreading through his chest. Just another night.

Headlights sweeping through the steamy glass in the front windows startled him. He slipped his pint under his laundry bag; maybe it was the lady who owned the place. She didn't want him drinking here. He kept his head down over his magazine. He could always sit in his truck if she chased him out, but he liked the smell of soap and the warm, lighted room. With relief he saw a young woman come to the door, try the knob, and then go back to her Ford for her laundry. So he was safe.

Wearing an army parka too big for her, she backed in carrying one full basket propped up on top of another. He didn't get up to help her. When she went back to her car for another load he took a quick swig of his brandy. He could tell from the quick, tight way she shoved her baskets around that she was intent on her work and wouldn't pay any mind to him and his pint. He went back to thumbing through the magazine.

She pulled off her parka and dropped it on an empty washer. Under, she wore a blue shirt untucked over her jeans. Her brown hair was loose and touched her shoulders. She had gold hoops in her ears but no makeup. It annoyed him that she'd plucked her eyebrows but hadn't penciled in a line; women who did their faces should keep them that way, otherwise there was something unprepared and helpless there, like coming up on a man who had his pants down. She wasn't very old, a lot of girls her age didn't make up at all, but she should have done her eyes. It was Saturday night, for god's sake; a woman should do up a little on Saturday night.

He poured another cupful. If she squawked about his drinking he'd put her straight right away—public property. He had rights. Women always try to run things. But somehow he liked to have her moving around, tossing clothes into the row of four washers she'd chosen. Maybe she'd hum or sing the way the girl did who cleared and washed up at the ranch. He liked hearing her sing country songs while he and the others were finishing up their coffee. It was nice to hear a girl's voice when she didn't know anyone was listening to her.

But this girl didn't sing; he'd stopped thinking of her as a woman, her face too round, her wrists too thin. She counted out her quarters and measured a cup of soap powder and a cup of bleach into each washer. He smelled urine from a washer full of diapers. She was old enough to have kids, then, though she had a teenager's awkward way of standing, one hand backwards on her hip. Hard out here for a girl with little kids. Nothing to do but raise kids and cook, the men out all day with cattle and crops. Not even a meeting hall in Pinedale. And the winters aged women fast, dried them out. This girl probably married her high school boyfriend and had kids right off. He cradled his pint against his belly. Well, she was going to let him alone.

As though she were all alone in the place, she sank down in a chair at the end of the row of washers and pulled a paperback from her purse. When she pressed open the book he saw with surprise that her hands were pale and soft and she had light pink polish on her nails. The girl who cleaned up at the ranch had blood caked around her nails already. So this one looked after herself some in spite of her kids. Then why didn't she make up her face? Lips thin, turned down like a little kid's, chapped. He couldn't figure it.

"You don't live around here." He surprised himself.

She looked up, startled, her earrings swinging against her neck. "What do *you* know about it?" He heard in her voice that she was even younger than he'd thought, maybe not even twenty yet.

"I'm not pointing a finger." He tried to smile but his face felt tight. He hadn't meant to talk to her at all and now she was mad. "I just notice things."

"Don't you go noticing anything about *me*." Her lips were a white line. "That's my car. I bought it."

He put his feet on the floor and leaned toward her. "Why, I didn't notice your car at all." What was she scared of? "I just notice things. Like your hands."

"And what about my hands?" She made fists, thumbs inside.

"Hey, now." He didn't know how he'd got into this, but he wanted out. Why did he talk up at all? He took a deep breath. "I didn't mean *nothing*. I just saw you had pretty hands. Women around here can't keep their hands pretty once they got kiddies and such." This time his smile came off better. "Just an old cowpoke paying attention. Nothing to trouble you about that."

Her eyes were wide and bluer than her shirt. A quick wash of tears came up.

"Come on, now," he said. "Don't take it serious. I just saw you're a young momma with pretty hands. That don't need to hurt none. I'm sorry I spoke up."

She didn't blink back the tears. Her eyes stayed fixed on his and he knew she was seeing him through a haze. She didn't have manners, to stare so. He felt unshaven, dirty, even though he showered and shaved that afternoon. She was looking at him too hard. He'd have to go sit in his truck after all. "Sorry. That's all I got to say."

She didn't look away.

What to do? He held out his bottle. "Got some brandy here. Make you feel better."

She shook her head, looked down into her book.

The hell with her, let her brood. He felt like throwing his chair at the wall. He'd been at peace, even content. Now he didn't know whether to stay or go. If he walked out she'd think he was mad at her; if he stayed he'd spend the next hour tippy-toeing around. She took up the whole room and her silence was louder than the washers whooshing.

"I'll take that brandy."

She didn't get up. He crossed to her and poured her some. Her hand was shaking, her palm, soft and pink. No wedding ring. "Drink up."

She sipped. "I'm just tired, I guess."

He sat down again, easier. Maybe she'd run off with a fella; maybe he'd left her with a kid. Well, he didn't want to know any more. He opened his magazine and pretended to read. In a few minutes it would be time to move his laundry to a dryer, and then it would be natural to pull on his coat and leave for a while. He could play the radio in his truck.

But she picked up her purse and her stack of dimes and came over to sit by him. She crossed her legs. She wore a man's boots, too big for her, worn at the toes. "I'm sorry," she said. "You seem real nice. I'm just plain jumpy and that don't have nothing to do with you."

"Just a mistake." He looked down at his magazine, his hands, knuckles knobby with arthritis, scars on his palms from roping.

"You got a finger gone. You been working with machines, right?"

"I lost that finger roping Brahmas. Got my hand caught in the rope and the bull fell on me. Eleven years ago. Then I quit the circuit."

The girl leaned back in her chair and held out her cup.

He poured.

"I see by your face you had a hard time." Her eyes narrowed now, tearless.

"Sort of." He wished she'd go now. He listened for his washers to snap off, but the rinse water was still churning. He took a drink of brandy like it was coffee, his mouth numb, his nose full of alcohol and fruit. "Everybody has hard times. That's the one thing I know."

He could see the clean, pink line of her scalp where her hair was parted. She looked up at him sideways, both her hands around her cup. "You were nice to me." She didn't smile. She drank what was left in her cup.

If he poured her another, they'd have the pint finished before their wash was in the dryers. He calculated the expense of talking with her. Only a faint flush had come up on her cheeks. "After I had to quit the circuit I bought me a string. Nice quarter horses. Bought them young, broke them myself. When I called them they came. But you can't make nothing out here on dudes." That part was true at least. "I sold the whole string but one and got work as a hand."

She was looking up at him over the rim of her cup. "You wish you could get clean away. Your feet are running while you're talking."

Well, he was shifting his feet, marking the chalky cement floor. He leaned forward to get up and leave.

"Listen. They ain't my kids."

"What?"

"They ain't mine. He was married but she run off and left him with the two of them. One just two years and the other six months. He didn't tell me about that."

Everyone's got a story. He poured more brandy in their cups and leaned back, waiting. The unshaded bulbs spun when he glanced up.

"I met him in K.C. I was working at the Pavillon, short orders. He was cutting timber out here, he said. Things looked real good, he said. So I come along. Then I find out about the kids and all.

They'd been with his mom, but she didn't want them. She's got her a job. Now here I am . . ." Her voice trailed off.

It wasn't a long story but it sank him low. Everybody cheating on somebody. "Why don't you leave? Married or not, you can leave."

Tears again. She pleated the edge of her cup. "Married! He ain't even divorced from *her*. And I don't know if I'd have him if he was free."

"Then go ahead and leave." He sat up straight. Easy, if you put all your cards out on the table.

"That bastard!" She balled up the cup and threw it into the waste can on the other side of the table. "I love him."

His machines clicked off. He felt softened, lazy. His face was as warm as if he were sitting by a log fire. His hands tingled with warmth. The clean tops of the washers looked like new snow, reflected light. Then her machines clicked off, and she stood, pulled a cart over to her washer, came back with another cart for him.

"Can't get no rest around here," she said. "Got to keep moving."

The warm, wet clothes eased his pains as he dragged his things out of the washer. Aspirin upset his gut; better to have the ache in his hands than be laid up with a sick belly. His load was small compared to hers.

She sorted her diapers and white things into one dryer, her colored things and towels into the next one, leaving two for him. "You be needing these both?"

He smiled. "Nope. I throw it all in together. If I keep putting in the dimes, sooner or later they're dry."

"Then I'm going to use this one for undies."

She pulled handfuls of panties out of her load, soft colors, blue, yellow, pink, tiny as handkerchiefs. Then came the bras the color of bare skin. He slammed the door of his dryer, thrust three dimes into the slot, one after the other, and sat down again. The magazine blurred, pink, yellow, and blue pages. The brandy was like July sun on his feet, his legs, his groin.

He looked up when she came to lean toward him across the folding table. An edge of a skin-colored bra was at the open throat of her shirt. She winked—straight, unpainted lashes, no eyebrows. "Sure do wish we had some more of that good brandy. Makes an evening pass, don't it?"

He pulled out his pint and looked at it in surprise: empty. With the color up in her cheeks she seemed younger and more rested. "Ain't you had enough? A little thing like you?"

She smiled as though he'd complimented her. "It don't hurt me. But I don't smoke. It stains your teeth." She parted her lips wide to show him her white teeth, the two upper incisors pushed out like a cat's.

He stood up without deciding he would and started for the door, pulling his coat from the hook by the change machine. "I'll get us a little more, then, since it agrees with you so good. You watch my clothes real close. Don't want nobody to steal my jeans." As he started his truck he saw her blurred by the steamy glass, her face rosy and small. She was looking toward the door after him. She couldn't see him, he knew that, but he waved.

The road to the highway was rutted, full of potholes. He rolled down the window and let the fresh air pour in smelling of pines and hay, damp earth. He didn't slow down coming off the gravel. An old cowboy looking for a thrill—even a skid is better than nothing. The truck slid onto the concrete and a jack rabbit bounded away through his lights.

He liked to hear the jacks scatter up by a horse's hooves, the swoop of an owl come close like the hiss of an arrow. He could sense deer, even if he couldn't see them—an extra sense of some kind. Lots of cowboys didn't have it but he'd hunted a good bit when he was on the circuit. Most men don't even hear the sound of their own footsteps. But he did. He noticed things. He was still smiling to himself. Drunk, he thought. Was he? Well, why the hell couldn't he feel good now and then? Any law against that? He pushed his hat back with his wrist and leaned his elbow in the open window.

There was a mob of cars around the Cowboy Bar, heads in the back seats of a couple of them. As he waited at the stoplight he heard the music when the door swung open, "somebody wrong song." He gunned her when the light changed and charged in behind the Liquor Drive-in again.

"What the hell's the matter with you?" Verna asked him as she handed him another pint out the window, taking his crumpled fiver. "You're looking gassy."

She didn't know everything. "Feeling fine. Feeling fine."

"Finished the other already?" The light bounced off her glasses.

"You ain't my old lady," he laughed.

"You're telling me." She grinned at him. "What's got into you?" She smoothed the collar of her white blouse and lifted her magazine to fan her face.

He saluted her with a snap of his wrist as he pulled away, his tires kicking up gravel.

The lights of the town fell away behind him the way shadows do when you come out of the woods into a meadow: they touched his hands, slid from his shoulders, then disappeared. A red moon hung low on the horizon. He could see the shapes of hills, softened and rolling, though they were steep and rocky enough by day. The shadows on them looked like fur, thick, without shine. The air on his face felt like water.

But his lips were parched. He sensed it coming on like a wild animal in the darkness near him, his skin prickling. It was under his ribs, at the back of his throat, in his groin, even in his hands. He gripped the wheel as hard as he could, groaning. Oh, god. He'd been without for so long he'd almost forgot, hoped he could forget. The need for a woman scared him, ate at his bones, his spine turning to water. He saw the way he was, a lonely, horny man, driving hell bent for leather towards a tiny coin laundry lit up ahead of him on the plains like a Christmas ornament: a fool in a hurry. He pushed down to the floor and the truck skidded tail around onto the gravel road. Maybe he'd turn it over in the ditch. He swung a full circle, scattering gravel into the scrub pine. Kill himself — a goddamn hero's death. But he straightened her up and made it to the coin laundry.

Empty? But her car was still there — Missouri license plates. Where was she? Then he spotted her sitting by the table, her forehead on her arms. He slammed open the door. "Howdy!"

She didn't raise her head. He unzipped his coat and pulled his chair up by hers again, but closer. He wanted to touch the little bones in her spine, a row that led down the back of her neck and into the collar of her blue shirt. "Hey, asleep?"

She turned to him then and he saw that she was unsteady, her eyes wide and dark, smudges of fatigue under them. "I been thinking about that song," she said.

"What song?"

"Ain't heard it at home for years, but they play it all the time out here." She sang, her voice lower, huskier. "I seen fire and I seen rain, and I seen lonely days I thought would never end, but I always thought I'd see you again."

He caught sight of himself in the window, a big-shouldered man with a squared-off head, white eyebrows, lines crowding his face.

"Don't know who I'm missing, but it's somebody. I been sadder out here than I ever been in my life. I just couldn't wait to run away from home, couldn't wait to go off with him. Now, I think, who did I think he was? I don't even like him, and here I am loving him, or something I made up about him. Loving that, maybe. Not him, after all." She sighed, sat up straighter. She had some fresh paper cups. "You bring that brandy?"

He filled two of them.

She settled back and put her free hand on his knee. "You know where I went today? I drove out to the gorge. We stopped at the Royal Gorge, in Colorado, on the way out here, and after that one this here gorge ain't much. But it feels the same. The wind whips up at you and it makes you dizzy to look down. Do you know, all the time I was scared I might jump off. Leave those kids in the car and just jump. When I got near the edge my heart nearly knocked me down." She put her hand on her left breast.

"But you didn't jump. So there ain't no reason to be scared."

"It was like a test for me. See if I would choose to live or die."

Carefully he patted her hand, let his settle over hers, pressed the warmth into his thigh. Heat radiated up his leg. "You can talk to me."

She nodded, then she shrugged. "Well, I found out one thing. I *don't* want to live like I'm living now."

She swallowed her brandy, her throat working with the gulp. She didn't even bother to taste it. He poured her another cup with his left hand, spilling a little on the table.

"Those clothes are about through." She gestured toward the dryers, taking care not to spill her brandy, though her arm swung wide.

"Mine have a long time to go." He figured three dimes, about thirty minutes, and he'd been gone fifteen, back maybe ten. They'd be shutting off soon. He scratched at his throat. She drew her hand back a quarter of an inch, just enough for him to notice. It was like hunting: you had to listen and watch. You had to keep a cool head. "The lady who runs this place, she don't like drinking. Let's us go out to my truck until the dryers stop, so she don't happen by to close up and get all huffy."

She closed her eyes, shook her head slowly, leaning against his shoulder. "Can't even have a drink where you want out here. I always drank at the Laundromat at home. Chablis. Kept the bottle in my clothes basket. No one said nothing." She stood up before he did and held out her arms so he could help her on with her parka.

Then she whispered, "Course *he* might come looking for me. I left him a note I went home to K.C., but I had to tell his ma where I was to get her to keep the kids."

"Looking for you?"

"He's terrible jealous. He was of *her,* too, but it didn't stop her from running off."

"Why'd you tell him you was going home?"

"That's what I *felt* like doing. I wanted to let him know. I wanted to make him sit up and pay attention."

Her parka smelled of smoke and talcum. He maneuvered her out the door, holding the cups on his fingers and the bottle snug in his pocket again. Then he settled her in beside him, and backed the truck across the parking lot, pulled into the shadows under the pines. The moon was down and the sky was streaked with turquoise light along the horizon. It was too dark to see her face, but his hand found her cheek. "Here we are." It was wet. He'd never kissed a crying woman. Her teeth caught his lips and his chin, but she put her fingers on the back of his neck and pulled him close, choking on her tears. He felt her breasts against his arm. "It's okay, honey," he said against her mouth.

"It's not. I don't care."

He slid his hand into her armpit under her coat, the side of his palm against her breast. Her tongue was at his lips even though she was crying and he got her bra up and found her wide, flat nipple.

Dizzy, like the time he and his horse went down in the river, water rolling them over and over against the logs, the stones, dark water over and under, turning and pushing him, and the blows of his horse's hooves against his legs. He wanted to get her on his lap, across his thighs. He pulled her against him, set her head on his shoulder. "You had a hard day." The words were huffs of breath in the dark. "Take it easy, honey."

Her hand let go of his neck and came to rest limp on his shoulder. He felt her wiping her face against his T-shirt. He began to rock her, moving back and forth from his hips, keeping her close. After a while a small snore came from her. He kept rocking. Her whole weight was against him. He fingered her nipple carefully, learning the surface, the tight bud at the tip, to remember later when he was alone.

Then the idea came to him: he would marry her. He had enough put back for a start, and if she worked, too, they could get by pretty good. Buy her a washer, a dryer. Her breath was steady and warm on his chest, like a puppy curled there below his chin. He could make things right for her. She would cook for him, sing her tuneless songs, and kiss him with her tongue.

Then a sweep of lights came down the road and a blue Chevy wagon pulled into the lot right up by her Ford. Dust puffed up from under the wheels and sailed up white around the guy who jumped out. Work shirt and work boots, yellow hair flashing under the neon light. He looked into the Ford, opened the driver's door and looked again. Then he walked stiff-legged into the coin laundry — maybe drunk, maybe angry.

In a minute he was outside again, looking around the lot, shading his eyes with his hand. Not such a tall guy, Matt judged, but big-armed like timbermen.

Then he jumped in his Chevy and backed it up full speed across the lot, gravel cracking, white dust spouting all around. Dust boiled onto the hood of Matt's pickup. The wagon stopped right in front, blocking his way. The man's face showed at Matt's window — a thin face, eyes too wide apart. When he wrenched open the door, Matt slumped toward him for a second, then pulled himself with a grab at the wheel.

"Bitch!"

She was awake, screaming. "I was going home! I want to go home!" And a long scream like a siren.

Matt pushed her back, swung the door shut, almost catching the man's hand in it, locked it, reached to lock her side, too. The man jumped onto the running board, reached in the open window and grabbed her by the hood of her parka. Easily, as though he'd been practicing, Matt got a shoulder with his left hand and even with the girl in his way smashed into the side of the yellow head with his right fist.

She was crawling over him, clawing, pushing. He tried to grab her arm. She sank her teeth in his hand. "Bastard!" She had the door unlocked and scrambled over and jumped out onto the gravel. She bent over. "Sweetie," she moaned. "Sweetheart."

After they drove off, he didn't bother folding his clothes. Sometimes he did, but tonight he grabbed them and stuffed them into a plastic bag. He slammed the door of the coin laundry behind him.

He didn't have to drive back through town. The road to the Circle C twisted west and north. The air was cold now, the wind coming off the hills. Over the motor he could hear the coyotes barking, the nighttime lowing of the herd. When he sighted the herd he pulled off the road and killed the lights, shut off the motor. Without the moon the herd looked like water moving in a dark current. It was a good herd; he'd tended it often enough to know. They'd lost a lot of calves, though. Spring was late and the end of winter bitter. The cows took their calves down into the stream beds to shelter them, and then stepped on them, pushed them down, trampled them in the stream when the last and worst storms came. It wasn't just the runts that drowned, either; fine, big bull calves went, too. No way in the world to save them.

He climbed out of his truck to walk toward the herd. Three hundred head here, at least. Their swaying backs stretched out before him like the plain itself flowing toward the draw. To his right he heard the stream, only four feet across up here, but full of trout, the water sweet and cold. He walked to it thinking to bathe his face. On both sides the cows parted before him, moving aside as he reached for them. He smelled the good cow smell of grass and manure. Their breath fogged at their mouths as his did. As he passed them he rested his aching hands on the comforting heat of their flanks, felt their muscles moving slow and solid. In the dark their white faces floated toward him as though through deep water. Their great, dark eyes, as blank as dreams, gazed at him until he shut his, and in blindness found his way to the stream by the sound of water over stone and the smell of the snow that was already settling on the mountains to the north.

The Trail to the Ledge

Gail wasn't in their cabin at Camp Berry, but she'd left a note for him taped to the refrigerator: "Took the jeep to get some groceries. Back soon. Your wife, Gail." They'd been married for six weeks and Gail got a kick out of calling herself "your wife." Jim pulled the note off and laid it on the drain board by the little sink as he opened himself a can of soda. Her big scrawled letters took over the whole piece of torn notebook paper. In the narrow space below her name she'd made large X marks for kisses. A little kid's writing, he thought. But she was twenty. He held the chilled can against his forehead a moment and then settled down at the pine table, glad to be alone.

He was the tennis coach this summer, with the kids from eight in the morning until dinnertime. When he got back to their cabin in the counselors' section, Gail was usually waiting for him. She was teaching drama and dance and wanted to talk about her day and to hear all about his. They'd taken the jobs at the camp so they could share their experiences, she reminded him. She'd found the openings in the Sunday *Times* and applied right away—two sheets of notebook paper in her big scrawl. Within a week they received a phone call. Their backgrounds were excellent and the director liked the idea of a married couple. It would add stability, he said, to the camp situation for the younger campers.

Jim opened the latest copy of *Sports Illustrated* and took a gulp of his soda. There was a good article on Conners. Studying Conners's follow-through on his serve, Jim could see Conners controlling the ball with spin. He turned his wrist like Conners to confirm his guess and heard the jeep pull up by the cabin door. Gail beeped the horn twice and he went to the window. She'd tied her hair back with an orange scarf and was wearing her green croupier's eyeshade for sunglasses. She'd left her really wild stuff packed away so they could fit into the camp atmosphere better, but she was wearing one of the tie-dyed T-shirts without a bra. He could see her dark nipples through the lavender cotton. He'd told her several times that he didn't think that was a good idea with so many young boys around.

"Want help with the groceries?" he called.

"Nope. I can manage, hon." She swung out of the jeep and grabbed a bag in each arm. Her hiking boots were loud on the bare planks of the cabin porch. He held the screened door open for her and she made kissing noises at him as she passed. "Little hick grocery. No fresh stuff at all." She dropped the bags on the narrow shelf by the sink and flung herself down in the canvas sling chair, pulled her scarf off and shook her head so that her thick, dark hair fell free around her face. She reached for his soda and took a long drink.

"I'm not especially hungry anyway," he said. After he'd finished coaching he'd gone over and swum in the large pool. It felt good to him to count the laps of his freestyle, to feel the water cold on his sunburned arms, his legs and back getting tired. For a while he forgot he was working at the camp; he was lost in the body memory of working for his senior lifesaving exam when he was sixteen. The other swimmers gave him cookies one of the mothers had sent; swimmers were always sugar hungry. He felt pleasantly guilty eating the heavy cookies, licking icing from his fingers, knowing he wouldn't want supper.

She bent to unlace her hiking boots. "How was your day, Jimmy?"

"Good. A good day."

"I think we're settling into the routine. My little princesses have gotten used to working their tails off."

"You had a good day?" he asked politely, watching her finish his soda.

"We did some truly creative stuff in the drama group. I had them act out life situations. One gutsy girl, the blonde I told you about, took the part of an alcoholic. Wow, was she *in* it. Really transformed herself. I was so proud!"

She settled back, stretched, and tipped her chin up to laugh with pleasure in the memory of her student. For a moment he saw her as he liked her best — clothed in the sheen of her own animal energy. He admired her because she liked herself so well. He'd thought of himself as second-rate most of his life. It made him feel free and good to be with her when she was enjoying her own enthusiasm. He wanted to be like that.

Stripping off her knee socks, she wiggled her toes, rubbed her powerful dancer's feet, all muscle. "Tell me about your day." It was more instruction than question.

"No superstars," he said promptly. "Three, maybe four, really strong guys. One good girl. Hits her ground strokes deep and hard, comes to the net like a guy." He couldn't think of anything creative that they'd done. Just the usual routines. He always pushed himself to do a disciplined drill, his own kind of compulsive drive. He had to depend on routine and unfailing discipline because he had no natural brilliance. He guessed he coached the same way. Still, that kind of discipline steadied the really good players and the mediocre kids got better through the drills. There wasn't much to talk about there.

She watched him expectantly. After a while she said, "Maybe you'd like to invite your kids to have hot dogs with us here some night. I was thinking of having some of my drama kids over. We could play theater games and do some improv. Know each other better. What do you think?"

He shook his head. He didn't want to get to know the kids better. He spent all day with them, that was enough. What would they say to each other? He was an adult to them, not a buddy. He'd hated the phoney friendship of one of his own coaches and admired another who stood back from him, who stayed in his role. "I guess I really don't want that," he added, trying for candor because he knew she liked that.

"I hear you," she said at once. "You value your privacy and I admire that, Jimmy."

"I want to keep my distance."

"Right, hon. But you understand that I want to get closer to my students. We're different that way." She leaned toward him, her face flushed with intensity. She got excited when they talked about "real" things, as she called them—their differences, their feelings, who they were. "I love you for your sense of your own privacy," she added. "You're a complicated, simple guy."

She'd called him a "complicated, simple guy" the first time she'd pulled his face to her breasts. He guessed she was right; he didn't understand his complications very well, but he liked simple things. He liked making love and really good steaks. He liked his records. He loved tennis. And he liked silence. He'd begun to realize that he'd spent most of his life in silence. He liked it that way. "I guess I'm tired right now," he said.

She stood and stretched. "I'm going to take a quick shower before I fix supper. Would you get me one of our secret beers?" She leaned to pat his thigh as he reached into the back of the refrigerator. "Jimmy, you've got the most gorgeous legs in the world. My tall, blond, silent man! I married you for your legs." She took her beer and padded toward the bathroom, unzipping her cut-offs as she went.

They'd got married because she thought she was pregnant. She was on the pill, but she thought somehow she'd slipped. By the time she confirmed that this wasn't so, they'd planned a simple wedding and told their parents. She wanted his baby, she said. He liked that idea. He liked to hear her say, "Baby. *Your* baby, Jimmy." When she found she wasn't pregnant after all, she said, "It felt right. Let's go ahead." He was doubtful, but she was so full of purpose. She loved him for his aloneness. She said, "I need someone cool. And you need someone warm." His friends in his fraternity told him he was a lucky guy. They said she was something special. He thought they sensed she was somehow better than he deserved.

The thing that worried him the most now that they were married were the nights. Of course they'd made love a lot before—in his car, on her dorm bed, on blankets in the woods—but they'd never slept together all night.

Sleeping with Gail was a different thing, and it frightened him. She was neither tall nor heavy, but her weight tipped him toward the center of their bed. She seemed enormous and dark. Even asleep he was aware of her hips and breasts, of her feet tangling with his. Sometimes she woke in the middle of the night and wanted to talk. He wanted her to be quiet and cool, then. He wanted to sleep. Sometimes, when he felt especially anxious and couldn't escape her breath or the pressure of her legs, he took the quilt and lay spread-eagle on the floor by the bed. He told her that it was too hot to sleep and the breeze moved on the floor. She'd reach down and rumple his hair, but in a few minutes she'd fall asleep and he could move away from her hand. Somehow he hadn't counted on her being with him all night. Nothing had prepared him for the weight of a woman against his sleep.

And she slept naked. Her skin gave off a scent of her musk perfume and of her sweat. He could feel her body heat even if she were several inches away. He'd always slept in his briefs and a T-shirt. He asked her if she didn't want to let him buy her a nightie. But she said no. She'd always slept naked. Once, on their honeymoon, she'd asked him to sleep naked with her. He wakened in terror. For a moment he was unable to tell where his body ended and hers began. He felt he'd lost his outline, that he'd blurred, melted into her. He got up at once and put on his underwear. But he felt her heat even through the cotton, and if she moved to his pillow her loose hair stuck to his throat and his shoulders. He didn't know what he was going to do about the nights if he didn't learn to sleep with her.

Gail liked to read in the quiet time after the all-camp activities around the campfire in the early evening. He'd got in the habit of going down to the tennis courts and hitting balls against the backboard, enjoying the feel of a light sweat coming up again and the breeze chilly on the back of his neck. He thought the exercise might help him sleep. When he returned to their cabin it would be almost 10:30, and he'd take a quick, cool shower and embrace Gail while he was still wet. She said once that she liked that. She also said they must be careful not to get into a rut with sex. "I like counting on it," he said. It was good to have a pattern to his days.

Tonight she blew him a kiss as he started down toward the tennis courts. She was reading a paperback novel, absently lifting and smoothing the hair at her nape. He stopped in the doorway and looked back at her stretched out in the canvas chair, her tanned legs propped up on the railing. He'd managed to eat the scrambled eggs she'd fixed — enough, anyway. "You're a good girl," he said abruptly, surprising himself.

She smiled. "I love you to pieces and you know it."

He took a side trail down to the tennis courts in the valley below the cabins, checking in his shorts pocket to make sure he had the key to the court lights. He swung at the pine shadows with his racquet. He should build up his wrists more, he thought. He'd have more control if his wrists were stronger. There was no chance of his being a pro; it looked as if he'd end up in his dad's insurance business. But he'd like to play well. It was important to do something really well.

The court was like a rectangle of dark, unreflecting water. When he turned on the lights the pines lit up with an almost artificial green. There was only the sound of the whippoorwills and the steady thud of his tennis balls. No one had ever seemed to notice that he was here at night. The young girls — thirteen-year-olds — in the cabins on the hill above the courts laughed and teased each other until lights out; he knew he didn't bother them.

But once on the courts he was bored. Two weeks into the ten-week session and already he was bored. He was hitting strongly enough, but it was an effort for him to try to control the ball. Maybe he was just too tired. He'd try to get a nap before supper; maybe that would help.

When he lobbed a ball over the backboard and into the woods he decided to quit. He hadn't even broken a sweat yet, but it wasn't worth it. He switched off the court lights and stood still in the dark, letting his eyes get used to the night. It was good to be alone. He didn't want to go back yet. In the soft silence he could hear the girls laughing in their cabins.

Without really deciding, he started up the trail that led to the hill. It was farther back that way, but he hadn't been gone very long. He realized that he was walking very quietly. When he saw the cabin lights flickering in the pines above him, he made himself breathe more quietly, too. He remembered the delicious freedom of running through the summer nights as a boy, rhododendron slapping his arms, the backyards dark and deserted, bright figures looking out of lighted windows — unable to see him.

The trail led above the counselors' cabin for that section — Eagles' Roost. Of the three cabins for girls, the highest one was just below the rocky outcropping on which the trail ran. Here it was almost total darkness, but he made out the marker just off the trail — Cabin Three.

There was the flash of colored towels hanging inside the long screened windows of the cabin below the trail. He heard girls laughing. He crouched down on the path, the scent of hot pine needles rising to him. The canvas drop cloths that were the sides of the cabin had been rolled up to the top, and he could see the four girls sitting cross-legged on their cots. They wore panties and T-shirts and were eating potato chips. One of the girls was reading a letter aloud. When she paused, the laughter of the others rose through the yellow mosquito lights like moths, fluttery and without menace. He glanced back down the trail — no one coming. But to make sure that he wasn't discovered, he crawled off the trail behind a boulder and lay on his belly on the ledge of limestone above the cabin and opposite the screened sides. He was about ten feet from the cabin, but in the dark shadow of the ledge.

He watched them only for a few minutes. Not much happened, but he hadn't expected anything. He felt a diffused excitement; he was doing something he shouldn't be doing. That sense of danger made his senses alert and sharp. He thought he could smell the Noxzema one of the girls rubbed into her shoulders. He heard electricity crackle when another leaned to whip her brush through her long blonde hair.

At 10:15 the cabin lights blinked — the signal that there was one minute before lights out. The red-haired girl put away her letter, and, without speaking, the four turned away from each other to take off their shirts and panties and to pull on pajamas. He caught his breath when he realized that they chose to withhold themselves from each other's sight, each alone on her own bed, quickly stripping and changing, her back to the others. The red-haired girl faced him, her face childish and solemn. Her nipples were flat and pale and she had a pinky down between her legs. Her shoulders and hips were like a boy's. Then the lights went out and he heard them calling good night to each other in the dark.

He climbed back to the path carefully, moving as stealthily as he could. His heart was pounding and his face was hot. He had a tightness in his chest. He thought of the girls' innocent restraint. Boys that age grabbed at each other's balls and slapped each other with towels. He hadn't liked that. He didn't want to be grabbed and pushed around that way. These girls didn't touch each other roughly. Each one seemed singular, surrounded by a haze of light. He wondered if Gail would understand his feeling for them. Then he decided that he would say nothing. There was nothing really wrong about what he'd done. But the vision was something that belonged to him alone.

He felt as full of energy and as loose-limbed as if he'd been running. When he came onto their porch he took Gail around from behind and laid his cheek against the top of her head.

"Are you going to take a shower?" She looked back and up at him.

"I guess I won't, tonight. I don't want to wait."

She stood up quickly and hugged him. "Oh, wow."

After they made love and she'd fallen asleep, he untangled himself from her warm arms and laid the quilt on the floor. He rested on his back, arms behind his head, and thought about the girls in Cabin Three. He thought about the bones in their shoulders and how their skin shone under the yellow bulb. After all, they were very young and quick and shy.

In the days that followed he developed a routine he could depend on. He and Gail would have their early supper, and if she came back tired or was late, he cooked so that they wouldn't linger over it too long. He learned to make good hamburgers and hot dogs with cheese. "I can't decide which I like best," she said, "looking after you or your looking after me." He made sure to help her clean up the pans so that they wouldn't be late for the campfire activities.

Some nights the girls and boys from her drama group gave skits; some nights there was square dancing. He was intensely aware of the girls from Cabin Three, but he was careful not to look directly at them. They were always together; sometimes they even walked four abreast, arms around each other's waists. When they sat on a log near the fire he glimpsed their narrow knees glowing in the firelight. Two of the girls were blonde, one with braids and the smaller one with loose hair that she wore back in a band. The tallest girl had short, dark hair and dark down on her arms and legs. The red-haired girl was heavier than the others and seemed to be the leader. He didn't want to know their names.

After campfire he and Gail would share a beer and talk. He told her everything he could think of that he'd done that day. He surprised himself with the amount of detail he could remember. "I love the way you're sharing yourself with me," she told him, leaning toward him, her chin on her fists. Then he'd listen to her. He kept his eyes on hers and was careful to follow what she said in case she asked him how he felt about anything she'd been doing. He wanted to be good to her. She was a good person. By 9:30 he was frantic to get away.

He'd take his racquet and tennis balls and the key for the lights and start down to the courts. His mouth was always dry when he stood on the dark courts and heard the laughter from the cabins on the hill above, but he made himself hit for a while. He timed himself: fifteen minutes at least. Never less. It was part of his discipline. And it enhanced his anticipation. He imagined the girls settling down, brushing each other's hair. If he reached the cabin by ten o'clock, he could watch them for fifteen minutes before lights out. He was never late.

Lying belly down on the warm limestone ledge, he discovered that they had a very simple routine. Sometimes they tried on makeup, helping each other with glosses that made their lips look large and shiny. Sometimes they trimmed each other's hair. Usually there was a letter to read aloud or one to be written, and they helped each other think of witty things to say about camp food. The small blonde often did back-bends on her bed, looking straight at him through the screen, upside-down and unaware. Mostly they sat on their beds and talked. And every night when they undressed he held his breath as they turned from each other, stripped off the triangles of panties and their printed T-shirts. Each one was serious and composed, utterly alone in the simple task. In those moments they seemed to him to be shining, quivering like flames.

When the lights went out he crept back to the path. Usually his hands had stopped trembling by the time he reached their cabin. But sometimes he had to run for a while before he went back; he was too short of breath to explain in any other way.

He slept less well all the time. Even lying on the quilt on the floor often he couldn't fall asleep until he heard the earliest doves begin their morning song, the high note followed by the three sad, low ones. He knew that if he was discovered looking in on the girls, there would be a terrible scandal. But he also knew how harmless he was to them; all he wanted was that vision of their cool purity. Who would believe that? And he knew he was betraying Gail in some way that he couldn't quite understand. Lying awake, he either planned his next visit to the ledge by the cabin, or rehearsed the disaster that would fall upon him if he were discovered. The need to see the girls and the need not to be found out seemed two equal weights nailed into his chest.

Once, in the middle of the night, Gail reached down for him and he caught her hand before she touched his face.

"You're still awake?" she whispered.

"Yes."

"Want to talk, Jimmy? Bad dream or something?"

"No. My stomach's upset, I guess."

"Camp's over next week," she murmured. "I guess we're both ready for a change."

He lay listening to his heart speed up, a dull sound that drowned out the early birdsongs. He'd tried not to be aware that time was passing. His routine had seemed beyond time somehow. But camp would be over next week; he had to face that. He knew the pressure of his guilt would be over then. But he would lose the girls. He didn't want to be back at college in married housing with only the memory of the scenes inside the girls' cabin. The memory wouldn't be enough. What would he do then? The thought made him helpless. Before he could manage to fall asleep he decided that since it was the last week it would be all right to go to their cabin a little earlier, to give himself more time with the girls.

The next evening Gail was designing a stage set in her notebook and he could slip away earlier than usual. He didn't bother to go to the courts at all, but took the path directly to the cabin by the trail along the top of the ridge. It was a still night and the air smelled of hay and tamarack, reminding him of the time when he'd been a kid — not innocent exactly, but free both of such need and such duplicity.

Even before he reached his place on the ledge by the cabin, he realized something was different. Someone was crying. He moved into his position and discovered that it was the red-haired girl who was sobbing, her face in her hands. The taller blonde sat on the cot beside her, her thin arm around the red-haired girl's solid shoulders. The small blonde sat on her own cot, her chin on her knees, rocking back and forth. The dark-haired girl lay face down on her own cot, sniffing. Had they been fighting? He'd never heard them raise their voices to each other.

Listening intently, he began to decode the bits of conversation. The girl's dog had been run over; her mother had written to tell her so she could be prepared when she came home and didn't find her dog there. The tall blonde ran her hand up and down the crying girl's back. Perhaps that was how her own mother comforted her. The crying girl bent double and wouldn't be comforted.

He'd never wanted to touch the girls before. He'd wanted them to stay remote and lovely. But now he felt a powerful urge to enter the cabin and take the crying girl in his embrace. He wanted to run his hands down her freckled arms, rest her head against his chest. He loved them all in some way he hadn't known. He didn't want any harm to come to them. He felt removed from them but powerful. If he went inside to her now, he'd know how to comfort the crying girl. After all these nights of watching, he *knew* her. She was more than the pure and wavering spirit he'd seen at first. She was an unhappy child. His throat was tight and he knew he must go back to his own cabin in case he moaned out loud. He had to think about this new feeling.

When he turned and started to crawl back up the trail he realized that there was somebody standing by the boulder and looking down at him, a shadow form. In the moment before she spoke he saw that it was Gail.

"I chased you. You forgot your court keys," she whispered, and then she began to cry.

She ran down the trail back to their cabin. He ran after her, afraid that he would catch her after all. After the first wave of guilt he had a burst of gratitude toward her; if she'd found him out at least no one else would discover him now. And then a flood of anger—

after all, what had he done wrong? It was her fault, somehow; she shouldn't have followed him.

When he reached their cabin she was crying hysterically, hunched down in the canvas chair. He'd never seen her cry before and the violence of her sobs frightened him. He sat down across the table from her and said her name but she wouldn't look at him. Her face was red and blotched and he saw that her eyes would be swollen. She had snot on her upper lip and she didn't try to wipe her face. He got her some tissues but she wouldn't take them from him. Then he got a washcloth dampened with warm water and she took that, burying her face in it. His hands shook worse than hers. He said her name again, but she kept her face in the washcloth.

"Is that part of your bag?" she asked through the cloth. "Little girls?" She started sobbing again but he was afraid to reach for her. Her whole body shook and she looked at him wildly over the blue cloth. "You'll get in trouble, you know that? They'll put you in jail."

When she was quieter he tried, "I don't know what it is, but it's over. It's all over."

She shook her head, staring at him. "I don't know what it is either, but it's not over. Not until we both understand. Not until we work it through."

"I can't talk about it."

"But I want to understand. I *have* to." She wiped her throat with the cloth and flung her hair back over her shoulders.

He rested his forehead on his fists. The pine table smelled of bacon grease, of the comfort of mornings. He closed his eyes, a constriction in his throat. "It's nothing. I just watch them for a few minutes. That's all."

"Every night?"

Before he realized that she couldn't have known that, he said, "Yes. Every night."

"Oh, god!" She started to sob again. "You've got to tell me! What's going on?"

"Nothing's going on." He didn't want to look at her anymore, her face red and her mouth slack from crying.

"Maybe it's nothing you have words for, but something is going on." Her silver earrings swung crazily, reflecting the overhead light.

"What hurts me the most is that you have this secret," she said softly, as though to herself. "It's not the little girls so much. It's the *secret*. Do you see that?"

He shook his head. Nothing he could tell her would be enough. She reached for his hand and he suddenly found himself furious with her. She'd followed him, after all. Spied on him! Now she wanted to turn his vision inside out, make it something that it wasn't at all, possess that as well. He jerked his hand away from her. "What about my privacy! You said you loved my sense of privacy!"

She jumped up, her hip hitting the table. "I didn't mean from *me!* That wasn't the agreement!"

"Your agreement. Your rules. Yours!"

She ran into their bedroom. He heard her opening drawers and in a short while she came out with her satchel. She'd washed her face and tied back her hair. She looked exhausted but she'd put on eyeliner. "I'm going to stay in town tonight. I've got to think things through. I just can't get hold of this."

He realized that he was relieved. He wanted her to go. He was very, very tired, but maybe he could sleep if he was alone in the bed.

"We've got to talk about this in the morning, Jimmy. We've got to understand each other. It'll finish us if we don't." She turned, started out the screened door, a moth darting around her head.

He moved after her, thinking he would tell her that he'd give it a try. But he found to his horror that he'd picked up an empty beer can and had hurled it at her back. She ducked beyond the screened door and ran toward the jeep. The can hit the screen and bounced back by his feet, leaving a trail of beer. "Bitch!" he yelled at her as she started the jeep. "Leave me alone, bitch!" He didn't want her to come back later and catch him crying.

A New Life

Ronna told Kristin that it was time for them to give up caffeine, to cut down on grass, wine, french fries, to shape up, join a gym. In fact, to join The Limberyard, which was right down the highway from Kansas City Mutual Insurance, where they both worked in the mailroom. "Now's the time," Ronna said. "The big three-O is coming up for us both. We've got to save what we can before it's too late." Kristin thought maybe it was already too late. Ronna insisted. "We've got to take control here as a team." Kristin let Ronna talk her into buying a shiny black leotard and black tights just like Ronna's. "Wonderwomen," Ronna said, and signed them up for a trial run at the gym.

"I'm too skimpy for this gear." Kristin pulled a strand of her blonde hair across her lips and tasted balsam. Without looking in the mirror, she knew that her shoulder blades and the sharp bones in her hips stuck out. "There aren't any men here, are there?"

"What guy would come to a place called The Limberyard? Too bad, you could show off your classy rear." Ronna patted her own. "Mellow out now, and let's pump some iron."

Dressed in her new gym outfit and her old running Nikes, Kristin followed Ronna into the mirror-walled gym, where the thick, warm air smelled of sweat and a gardenia-scented chemical deodorizer. Over the loudspeaker a Ramones tape howled. A gray-haired woman in faded blue sweats and a red bandanna pumped a chrome machine known as a pec-deck. A tall woman hauled down the bar of the tricep-pushdown; her narrow nose and thin lips reminded Kristin of her mother's face, though Kristin could imagine the disdain her mother would have had for this place. The women on her mother's side had lived on farms and raised large families; they worked, they didn't work out. But, like Ronna, these women in the gym seemed full of energy and purpose. Maybe Kristin would catch it.

"Where do we start?" Kristin said.

"Don't you love it?" Ronna flung herself onto the sit-up bench. Her face was flushed, her forehead and arms gleamed as if she'd already been exercising.

Kristin crouched in front of the squat machine. She slipped her shoulders under the padded bar, as she'd seen the woman in the bandanna do, but when she tried to stand her legs trembled.

The gym instructor's husky command came from somewhere behind her. "Blow the weight up, honey. Breathe deep, then blow out."

Kristin blew, pushed, stood. It was a small victory, but she needed it. Anyway, this would be something to do. She wanted to keep busy, very busy.

After their workout, Kristin and Ronna showered, dried off, then sat in the sauna. Ronna squeezed water from her thick, dark hair onto the sauna floor. "I can't resist joining up, can you?"

"Something about it depresses me."

"Everything depresses you. You are basically a depressed sort of chick. That's what I'm trying to spring you out of."

"I don't like lying around in someone else's sweat," Kristin said.

Ronna tucked the top of her towel under her arm. "All you're talking here is damp orange vinyl. There's no place you can go somebody else hasn't already been, toots. We're all just passing around used goods."

Of course Ronna said that because her lover was married, but Kristin pushed her. "How about all *your* talk of a fresh start, then?"

"Everything is relative." She tossed back her hair and left Kristin alone in the pine-scented cave of the sauna.

By the time Kristin dressed and got upstairs to the desk, Ronna was already signing her contract, the instructor in her pink sweatshirt looking on. "Can't you hurry a little?" Ronna said to Kristin. "It's *Tuesday,* remember?"

Maybe it was because Ronna rushed her that Kristin signed her maiden name to her contract. She had to study the name a moment to realize that it was hers, the way she was sometimes startled to recognize that troubled, pensive face in a store window as her own. Kristin McKenna—she let it stand. Why not, if she was beginning a new life?

Driving them in her Fiesta to the parking lot of Shopmore, Ronna broke the speed limit twice. She had arranged for Kristin to meet Gene today. After work one afternoon, over beers at the Laurel Tap, Ronna had confessed to her affair with him. He worked nights on the police force; his wife, Sally, worked half-days as a legal aide. So the only sure time he and Ronna could get together was late afternoon. "We're crazy about each other," Ronna said. "But of course it's awful hard for us to have any kind of normal relationship. For example, he'd like to meet my friends. You're the only one I think would understand. You're older than the other girls, experiencewise." As much out of curiosity as to please Ronna, Kristin had agreed to the meeting.

Ronna parked by the bags of peat moss and the flats of tomato and onion sets. The sweet, rotting scent of fertilizer bloomed in the April sun as they waited. Then a blue Chevy wagon pulled up nearby, and a man jumped out and made his way to them between crates of potting soil. He was wiry, with thinning brown hair, glasses, an inch of beard. His shirt-sleeves were rolled up, and across his chest in a denim baby sling rode a plump-armed blonde baby, cheek pressed against the work shirt.

"He's got a child?" Kristin said.

"He was going to leave her for me, but damn if she didn't get pregnant! It killed me." Ronna's chin puckered and a rash flared on her throat as though she would cry, but she called, "Hi, sweetie!"

Then Gene was at Kristin's window. She saw a reflection of her face swim on the surface of his glasses. After a quick, assessing glance, he reached past her to grab Ronna's outstretched hand.

Ronna made a kissing sound. "Meet my pal Kristin. This is Gene Jacobson."

"I've heard about you," he said. "Ronna says you're the greatest. You really looked after her when she got this job."

Kristin touched the baby's soft arm tentatively. "Who's this?"

"Tim. Six months of relentless energy."

She looked for a moment at the carefully trimmed line of Gene's moustache, and then the baby turned his head and fixed her with his solemn gaze. His pudgy fist closed on a loose strand of her hair. When he pulled her head closer, she inhaled a sweet mix of soap, baby oil, and clean baby sweat. Blue veins threaded under the translucent skin at his temples. "Hello, Tim," she said softly.

The baby's delicately arched lips opened, but he made no sound. With her hand, she encircled the small fist entangled in her hair. His fingers felt like miniature shrimps.

"He's crazy about blondes," Gene said.

"His mother's blonde," Ronna said. "So I've heard."

"Want to hold him?" Gene asked.

As though they'd rehearsed the moves, Gene opened the door and Kristin held up her arms; he slipped off the sling and handed her the baby.

"Hop in," Ronna told Gene. "Let's go get us a soft drink." Then he was in the back seat, his hand on Ronna's shoulder, and they were driving north past the beltline.

The baby lay on his back in Kristin's lap. When she bent over he grabbed her hair in both his hands. "Tim." The ping of his name on the roof of her mouth pleased her. Guiltily — why would she think such a thing? — she imagined laying her lips on his. She would taste the freshness of his skin.

When she glanced up again Gene was leaning forward and joking with Ronna about a guy on the force who'd been ordered to knock off twenty pounds.

Ronna had told Kristin that Gene was her hero. She lived with her mom, so to be alone she and Gene drove off into the country and made love in the wheatfields or under the cottonwoods by the river. When he could get away, now and then, for a whole afternoon, he packed them a picnic of smoked turkey, deviled eggs, and beer, and they went to a motel on the beltline. Sometimes they took fancy underwear for her, kimonos for them both, cowboy boots. He's a wild man, Ronna said.

Gene pushed up his glasses and rubbed his eyes as though his head ached. The bridge of his nose was sunburned and peeling. "How'd you get in the mailroom game, Kristin?"

"I was teaching third grade at St. Thomas, but I got laid off. Lewis, my husband, taught math in the high school. Math's more secure these days."

"Have you got kids of your own?"

"She was widowed. I told you that." Ronna cut a corner close to swing into the carhop section of an A & W on the outskirts of town.

"I'm sorry. I just thought she might have kids. She seems to like Tim." Gene dropped his glasses back into place. Through the lenses his eyes were larger, their blue darker.

"It's okay," Kristin said.

"Not all of us *want* kids." Ronna yanked off the lavender plastic headband that matched her T-shirt and tossed it onto the dash. "Three root beers," she told the carhop.

"Take it easy." Gene stroked Ronna's throat. "Hey, your hair's damp."

Ronna let her head fall back, trapping his hand. "We joined a gym today. If we don't look after ourselves, no one else will." She'd told Kristin that she had been on her own since high school. Before moving back home she'd hitchhiked all over the West, working in Arizona as a short-order cook and in Utah as a ranch hand. She had gone to a junior college for a semester but had dropped out. "It was all baloney," she said of her college days. "I don't know how you lasted so long, Kristin. It's all hot air. With a diploma and half a buck you can get a cup of coffee." It looked as if she were right. Here was Kristin, sorting mail too, and although Ronna had her adventures to look back on, Kristin had only five years of scholastic drudgery and three years in a tiny grade school. And Lewis.

Kristin leaned down over Tim again. He gazed at her without blinking. Something about the baby made her think of Lewis — Lewis at the last, anyway, in the hospital. He'd curled into the fetal position, his knees to his chin. Meningitis, the doctor said. When the resident brought his sterile tray to give Lewis a spinal tap, the instruments had spilled onto the floor. The syringe rolled under the bed. Kristin ducked down and took it in her hand; had they chosen this enormous one because Lewis was so tall? She wanted to ask, but she was crying, and the doctor told her to wait outside. After Lewis died, she decided she was through with love. The pain of it spread out around her on all sides, like deep water difficult to move through.

Tim pummeled her stomach with his kicks, waved his arms. Ronna finished her root beer and handed the baby sling to Kristin. "Since you two get along so well, how'd you like to take him in that park for a while so Gene and I can take a ride and talk things over?"

Gene looked down into his empty glass mug. If they had set her up, Kristin didn't mind. The small park next to the A & W was filled with young mothers in jeans and kids playing on the swings and the jungle gym. It was better than going back to her little apartment alone.

"Does he have a bottle?" As she asked, she realized she'd made a choice, though she wasn't sure what she'd chosen.

Gene handed her a quilted plastic shoulder bag. "Seems like you know what to do."

"You're a living doll." Ronna patted Kristin's thigh.

Letting herself out of the car, she forgot to ask when they'd come back. She turned, but Ronna was already driving off, white dust spinning up behind her wheels. It was Gene who waved goodbye.

She was alone with the baby. The wind off the plains tossed the silvery cottonwood leaves. On the benches under the trees the mothers chatted and laughed. One nursed her baby under her shirt. When Kristin walked over they smiled, asked about her child. He nuzzled her shoulder, the damp circle where his mouth rested growing larger. Watching crows fill the pines along the field, she leaned back on the bench, the baby's weight a radiant warmth across her breasts.

The late afternoon shadows on the wheatfield beyond the pines reminded her of the farm. She'd lain on the porch roof and pretended the house was a ship sailing across the waves of wheat. Her mother raised four children there. If you had a child to care for, days took shape, simplified, held their own meaning.

The baby slept, and perhaps she did, too, though she heard the voices of women and children all around her. When he woke she gave him his bottle of orange juice, cradling him across her lap as the woman next to her held her child.

When Gene called to her she looked up, startled. He came from Ronna's red car across the park. She got up quickly, slung the bag over one shoulder, cuddled Tim on the other. "Are you okay?" he asked.

She nodded. Perhaps she had slept; she felt dizzy—though maybe that was from the exercise and the fresh air.

"I mean about this babysitting. Ronna can be pushy."

"I can take care of myself."

But, as though she needed protection, he took her elbow and they went to join Ronna, who rested behind the steering wheel with her head tipped back. She blinked up at Kristin with a dazed, satisfied frown. "How's your little boyfriend?"

On Tuesdays and Thursdays after work Ronna and Kristin met Gene at Shopmore. If the weather was good, Ronna and Gene went off in his wagon, and Kristin took Tim in the Fiesta to the park. If it was rainy, she took him into Shopmore, pushed him slowly up and down the aisles, stopped to sit in the cafeteria section. There she held him on her lap and taught him to hang onto her fingers, to pull up. He pushed his face against hers, his lips on her cheek. Soon he'd be talking. She'd teach him the names of things, her own name. She bought a book, *You and Your Baby.* On Mondays and Wednesdays after work she and Ronna went to the gym.

Ronna was doing crunchies on the inclined board, her gold chain with its teardrop charm swinging behind her as she raised herself, elbows to her knees. She'd braided her hair. She looked Indian, tanned already, although it was only May. "I wish I still smoked." She watched Kristin sideways.

Her knees cracking, Kristin did deep knee bends with a weighted bar. "But look what good shape you're getting in."

"I need something for my nerves."

"What's wrong with your nerves?" Kristin didn't speak to Ronna of her own. Lewis had been dead for over a year now, but still she often woke before light, her heart crashing. Something was wrong, something that couldn't be fixed, but she was unable for an awful moment to remember. Then, when she *knew,* no matter how she tried to arrange the pillows, she was unable to sleep again. More than anything else, she missed sleeping with him, curled against his long back, her arm over his side, her knees tucked behind his. It had been such a safe place. These days she gave up, fixed her breakfast, and thought of where she might take Tim; maybe there was somewhere she could show him puppies, kittens, ducks, some of the animals she grew up with on the farm.

Ronna lay back and chewed on the end of her braid. Upside down her face looked childlike, unformed. Kristin kept up her slow rhythm of lifting while Ronna talked.

"Sally's giving Gene grief about what does he do with Tim, where does he go, who does he see. Gene says it's hard to get away. Not that Sally's so crazy about having a baby. 'You were the one who wanted him,' she tells Gene. 'You take care of him. He's yours.' So he says. When she got pregnant, she said she wanted an abortion. But he said he couldn't live with that. So now she expects him to take Tim all his free time. It's wearing him down. Like, he's just burned out on these quickie meetings of ours. I tell him we should get married. He says he *is* married. He says he'd like to build another room on his house for me! It's all such a dead end. At first I thought I'd do anything for him, like I'd lie down and die if he asked me. But I'm coming apart. What do you think, Kristin?"

Kristin didn't answer. A fist of anxiety blocked her chest. How would she see Tim?

Ronna reached back and grabbed Kristin's ankle. "Hey, don't be so sad for me. Wonderwomen, remember?"

When Kristin caught her breath, she said, "That's a comic strip, Ronna. I don't hear us laughing."

Kristin crossed the gym to ride an exercycle. She pedaled fast, pumping heat fiercely into her chest. She could bike all the way across the plains and over the mountains, a single, long, ferocious effort all this exercising and clean living had prepared her for. She could swing Tim onto her back and run away.

How had it happened that she loved this baby? She wasn't the kind even to notice other women's kids. The subject of children had barely come up between her and Lewis. First they'd had to get

through college, then they'd needed jobs. They spoke of a family
as something they'd attempt when they had some savings, maybe
even a place of their own. And, after all, they both worked with
kids all day. But none of those she'd taught had ever seized her heart.
Tim was the only one to do that. She loved a child who wasn't hers
and she wanted *him*. Not another. Oh, god.

On the way to meet Gene at Shopmore the next day, Kristin offered
Ronna the use of her apartment for their meetings. "It's homier, and
it's close by. You'll have more privacy. I put out clean towels."

Ronna teared up. "You are a goddamned sister, you know that?
What can I do for you?"

"Take some hamburger out of my freezer to defrost, if you think
of it. That's plenty. Let's not talk about it."

Ronna grabbed her hand. "I'll get Gene to start your supper for
you. He owes you, too, and anyway, he loves to cook. He should
have been a mother. When we go to a motel he always wipes out
the washbasin so the maid won't find it watermarked."

Kristin slid the house key into Ronna's shoulder bag. "You think
he'll go for this?"

"Will he ever!"

When Kristin let herself in that evening she smelled onions,
tomatoes, browned beef. Rice steamed in a separate pan. A damp
towel was folded and laid on the bathroom hamper. The bed was
made. Maybe it hadn't been unmade. Maybe they had spread the
quilt on the floor, as she and Lewis had done on summer afternoons.
She didn't want to think about it. She had enough beef and rice for
two nights, and reheated it tasted even better. On Thursday she left
chicken in the refrigerator and found a fricassee waiting for her.

Except for the delicious meals Gene made, and an occasional damp
towel, she never saw signs that they'd used her place. Of course, Gene
was a cop. Maybe he checked out the room, put everything back
exactly where it had been, and picked up after Ronna, who habitu-
ally left hamburger wrappers and soda cans on the floor of her car
until Kristin threw them into a dumpster. It was almost as though
they hadn't been there at all.

Kristin, Gene, and the baby waited in Ronna's car while Ronna ran into Shopmore for shampoo and hand lotion. The day was hot, and Kristin sat sideways in the back seat, her legs stretched out, Tim dozing in her lap. Gene watched Ronna hurrying between cars and vans in her denim skirt and red T-shirt; then he turned and slung his arm along the back of the seat. "That old photograph over your rocking chair. I like it."

It occurred to Kristin that she and Gene had never been alone before. "That's my grandma and her sister. That's her sewing rocker, too. They lived on a farm next to ours up north of here. I think of their place when I'm in the park with Tim. I remember the way the wind blew day and night, and the shapes of the clouds, like fat animals in the sky." That she had said so much surprised her. She looked down at the sleeping child in her lap, the pearly sweat on his temples.

After a moment Gene said, "The cut-glass pitcher is nice, too."

"That was a wedding gift."

"I don't suppose you want to talk about your husband."

"I don't mind." He hadn't asked about her life before; she liked it.

"You probably miss him a lot."

"I miss the way I felt with him."

"Which was?"

He was watching her so closely that she looked out the window at the stream of cars pushing along the highway. "Quiet, I guess. We worried about things, of course, but as it turned out they were the wrong things." Then, with alarm, she heard herself ask — either to change the subject, or because she wanted to know — "How do you manage all this?"

"You mean Ronna?" When he smiled he looked less tired, younger. "Two lives."

"It's pretty much a mess. I want you to know that I *know* that."

When she didn't respond, he went on. "I've made some dumb choices, but I'm not dumb."

The drone of the traffic was a dull roar like the wind. A line of clouds moved seamlessly across the rolling hills beyond the shopping center.

"We shouldn't have gotten you into this," he said.

"What you do is your own business."

"I mean involved with us. You're not the kind."

She wished he would look away. She felt color rush to her forehead and cheeks. "I'm not involved, actually." Was she? Was she an accomplice, as they said in the movies? And maybe, in spite of what he said, she *was* the type. If you want to know someone, you watch what they do.

"You're a sweet lady," he said. Then he reached to open Ronna's door for her. As Ronna pushed her bag into the front seat, he went on, "Who did you say you were seeing now?"

"She picks up guys now and then." Ronna winked at Kristin in the rearview mirror. "They go for tall, blonde types. Short, dark chicks like me don't do so well."

"You're doing fine," Gene said to her.

When Kristin got home that evening, she found a pan of brownies cooling on the counter.

"He says I'm doing fine, but I'm *not* doing fine! I'm doing lousy!" Ronna had cried for a long time in the parking lot outside The Limberyard. Now she was inside, doing sit-ups and sniffing.

Stretching her hamstrings, Kristin lay beside her on the orange and green flecked carpet. "If you don't feel so good, we could leave."

"Do you think I care if I cry here? Who do you think I am, anyway, to care about what other broads think? You think *they* don't cry? This is a totally rotten life, and you know it as well as I do." Her face was swollen and splotchy, but she kept at the sit-ups, her braids swinging.

"Take it easy."

"I knew this was going to happen, that's what kills me! I predicted it!"

"Predicted what, exactly?"

"What I haven't told you. Gene says he doesn't see how things can go on between us. He says there's too much guilt for him in this sneaking around. Suddenly it's guilt! Where was his guilt when he was so horny last winter? What he means is that it's over."

Kristin pressed her forehead to her knee and closed her eyes. She let her breath out slowly. "Over? Just like that?"

"Two years of my life, two years and a half, I've given to that bastard!"

"But how can it be over?" Kristin was afraid to look at Ronna. She looked instead at her own pale, triangular face in the gym mirror. Take it easy, she told herself. But she was scared. Her neediness made her light-headed. Her ears buzzed, as though she'd drunk wine on an empty stomach.

"Well, maybe it's not completely over. He says he'll meet me today to talk it through." Ronna pushed up on one elbow, tears running down beside her nose. "I know this isn't our usual time, but please say you can babysit."

When they met Gene at Shopmore, Ronna had herself under control again. After her shower she'd smoothed on herbal lotion and pulled on new underwear, skin-colored and shiny. She dried her hair under the blower and threaded gold hoops in her ears. "Hi, honey," she called to Gene.

"Looks like rain." He bent to Ronna's window. "Let's get going."

Clouds massed in the west. Wind blew grit up from the parking lot, flinging it against the windshield. Gene had Tim's head covered with a blue blanket.

When Kristin held out her arms for the baby, Gene asked, "Where will you wait out the storm?"

"Here. If it passes over, I'll go to the park." She didn't look at him; she watched the rosy, smiling face of Tim, who reached for her, clung to her neck.

Gene fastened the car seat he always brought with him now. Marks the color of the clouds slanted below his eyes, as though he'd had trouble sleeping. Ronna jumped out, holding her skirt down, and ran to the station wagon, her gold hoops swinging.

Through a film of dust coating her windows, Kristin watched until Gene pulled away. Ronna was shaking her head, gesturing as though tearing cobwebs. Like the roof of an army tent, the khaki clouds sank lower. But Kristin headed for the park. She wanted the open space around her.

In early June the side ditches were already choked with Johnson grass and cockleburs, the pine tassels releasing their pollen into the wind like green smoke. Now and then a shaft of sun struck through the boiling clouds to pick out the tin roof of a silo. She drove beyond the farmsteads and into the prairie, which seemed to move eastward under the wind. It came to her that she was searching for her own house, though the place had long ago been torn down. All that would be left was a well cover and a windmill in the corner of some wheat or corn field. And wasn't it farther out, almost to Cross Plains? She hadn't been there since they'd moved to town, her senior year in high school, but in her mind she clearly saw the weathered gray house with its long porch, the collie sleeping under the ragged lilacs, the copse of black alder where she and her sisters played dolls. In the side yard her grandmother, in a flowered cotton dress, swung a chicken around her head to wring its neck. In the flat light of the kitchen her mother blanched and peeled canning tomatoes, squeezing seeds into a blue-speckled bowl. They did not talk while they worked, and they worked all day and into the long evenings. They were sturdy, joyless women. What needs they'd had of their own Kristin had never heard acknowledged. They were women without illusions who could not abide ambiguity. How had her own life become so confused and uncertain? She turned the Fiesta around in a lane and headed back to the park.

When she reached it, she pulled into the empty lot and kissed the top of Tim's head where his blonde, downy hair was damp, laid her cheek there. She felt as though her ribs had cracked, each breath pushing a shard of bone into her lungs. She recognized the pain: she was mourning, whether for the baby or for her own lost clarity and sureness she couldn't decide. "Let's get going," she said aloud, and lifted Tim from his seat.

The wind was a strong, steady hand on her back. It pushed her toward the pines, and when she'd crossed the ditch there it pushed her out until she was knee deep in the green wheat. All around the earth stretched out like a firm floor, but she thought now that the ancient explanations were truer: although the world looked wide enough, if you weren't careful you could fall off the edge. Monsters would eat you. You had to be very careful, and who knew what precautions would serve? Tim hung onto the collar of her plaid blouse, his large eyes narrowed against the wind. "Never play with matches," she said to him. "Don't run into the street. *Remember.*" But who can be another's protection from the interior dangers, which can't even be imagined until suddenly they are right there, close enough to touch?

Rain spattered across the wheat like buckshot. As she turned to run back, she saw that Gene's station wagon was in the parking lot, and that he waited for her in the passenger seat of the Fiesta. She threw Tim's blanket on him, bent over him as she ran. By the time she leaped into the car, her hair was plastered to her head, her face was wet, water streamed from her bare arms. When she unbundled Tim, he started to cry irritably—wet, cross, and teething. She offered him to Gene, but he shook his head, so she bounced the baby on her shoulder. "Poor little fellow," she crooned.

Gene leaned forward on the dashboard, resting his chin on his arms. Mascara was smeared like an oil stain on his collar. He slipped his glasses into his pocket and pressed his fingertips to his eyelids. "I broke it off with Ronna. She wanted me to take her home. She said you could bring her car by later."

Her chest collapsed from letting out a long breath. She had to comb her wet hair off her forehead with her fingers in order to see his face.

He scrubbed his eyes with the backs of his hands. "I used to think of myself as a good man."

"It's a hard time," she said cautiously. Tim was quieting, sucking his thumb.

"I've hurt people. I'm sorry for that. I told Ronna I was sorry."

"I don't imagine that helped much."

He looked at her as if she'd slapped him. Maybe she had. "No, it didn't help. But I'm going to straighten things out."

"Sometimes life just won't straighten out." She spoke against Tim's head.

"You sound shaky."

"It's just I'm so tired." Rain flooded over the roof of the car, battered the puddles that had already made a pewter lake of the gravel lot. Wheat lay dark and flat all the way to the horizon.

"I'd feel so much better if I could help you, Kristin. You deserve help."

"I get along—"

"We'll go to your place, the three of us, and I'll fix us some dinner."

"Your wife—"

"She's at an office party. I bought some rib-eye steaks for us, and you can fix a salad. You've got lettuce and sprouts."

So he'd worked it out. All of it. She imagined the three of them in her small kitchen, Tim in his seat, she and Gene at the round table, their plates heaped with steak, mashed potatoes, butter beans. Rain would drip from the eaves, squirrels scutter across the balcony, night come slowly on. A happy family scene.

Tim began to cry again, banging his head against her shoulder. He wanted his bottle, his supper, and to be put to bed. In her apartment, she and Gene would be alone while the child slept. "It's late for him," she said.

"A quiet supper is all." As though he had lost his balance, he leaned to her suddenly and brushed her cheek with his lips.

Her throat ached—to be held again. To have the baby near. Gene's thumb traced her chin, radiating a complicated pain.

"I'll follow you back. Drive careful," he whispered. "We all need a rest."

He opened his door, letting in a gust of wet wind that smelled of onion grass and mint. But she caught his arm. Quick, she told herself. Quick! Don't think about it. She handed Gene the baby, began pushing his things into the plastic bag. Her hands shook as she unhitched the car seat.

"Take him to his momma!"

"You need someone, Kristin."

But she was shoving Gene now. "You don't know. You can't possibly know. Get going!" She was in a panic not to weaken. Get him out of here, get the baby out of her sight.

He stood half out of the car, Tim thrashing in his arms. "Just at least let me fix you your dinner. We'll talk."

"I'm not going back now. I'm going to sit here and watch the rain. Go home." She turned her face and heard him shut the door. She closed her eyes, clenched her teeth. In a minute, over her thudding pulse, she heard his car engine sputter, then catch. Don't look. Don't think. In a minute more they'll be gone. A rush of water and wet gravel retreated behind the motor sound. When she opened her eyes, she saw his taillights reflecting long red ribbons on the highway.

Tim's blanket lay on the floor of the car. She picked it up, pressed it to her face, then clutched it in her lap, nesting her hands in the soft folds. The summer storm was already passing, the shimmering curtain of rain wavering eastward like the northern lights. Behind the rain the broken clouds were the ochre of windfall pears. She eased down in the seat, studied the sky. She wanted to feel relief, or even moral certitude. But she felt neither wiser nor a better person, only more alone. After what seemed a long time, though it may have been only minutes, she pushed the key into the ignition. As she lifted her head, she caught sight of a row of towering cumulus that the lower-passing rain clouds now revealed. The great hump-backed shapes like camels, the setting sun bronze on their hindquarters, drifted over the drenched plains.

Inventing the Kiss

After Jo unpacked her suitcase, she took her high school yearbook, opened it to Kit's picture, and propped it up by the phone. It was hard to get his image back. While she'd been in Europe with her parents she'd wanted to miss him, but she really didn't know him well enough to miss him very much. Still, he'd almost kissed her that last evening before he left to be a camp counselor up in Wisconsin. She imagined Kit lying with his head in her lap, the way she'd seen some French students messing around. She would touch his lips with her finger, lean down over him, and he'd kiss her. She was eighteen and no one had kissed her yet. She called Kit's house.

His mom answered. "Jo who? Oh, yes, Jo Tull." Kit was back from the camp, but he was subbing for a lifeguard at the Fort Sheridan pool. He'd be home at eight and she'd tell him to call. Mrs. O'Rourke didn't seem especially pleased with the news that Jo was back home. "Want to leave your phone number?" she asked.

"Kit knows it," Jo said, wondering if he did.

The September sky was a pale lemon, black branches of the butternut like ink marks across it, when Kit pulled up in the old black junker of a Pontiac he'd bought with the money he made at his after-school jobs. Jo was sitting on her front porch, chilly in her sweat-jacket. She'd planned to wait until he came to the door, but she ran down to his car as he was getting out.

"Hey," he said.

His face and arms were dark with freckles and there was a line of zinc oxide on his lower lip where he burned the worst, a smear of it on the collar of his red shirt. He wore Levis and a pair of rubber thongs. Hadn't he been taller? He could have looked directly into her eyes if he'd look at her; he was looking at her house.

"I'm back." She patted the hood of his car.

"Great." Then he repeated it, more enthusiastically. "Great!" He studied the butternut tree at the end of the porch.

"So I called."

"Great."

"Were you expecting me today?"

"Sometime around now." He'd started to say "pretty soon," she thought, then switched when he stumbled on the "p." He examined the band on his waterproof watch, tightened it.

"Well, here I am."

The watch required more attention, was tapped and held to his ear. "Great."

She pushed her hands into the pockets of her gray sweatjacket and leaned against the fender. What had she expected? He would rush to her, take her in his arms. "The trip was okay," she said, as though he'd asked her. "But it wore me out. I guess I wrote you that, didn't I? Did you get my letters?"

He looked up then, smiled. White teeth, brown eyes the color of his freckles, a thatch of red hair bleached from chlorine. There was a gold chain around his neck with a small cross—that was new. "Yeah, you wrote that. You write good letters. The kids in my group talked me out of the weird stamps."

"Maybe I should have written directly to your campers!"

"No way." He reached to her just as she moved aside, their arms bumped and he drew his back.

She tugged at the collar of her jacket. "I wanted to sleep this afternoon, but I couldn't. I'm excited to be home. I don't mean excited like 'great,' but real spacy. Everything is different. You know what I mean?"

"Yeah." He reached again and took her hand in his.

The gesture wasn't a lot, but it warmed her. "Kit, you're really tan. Much darker than you were. That's different, too. You look like a surfer. Do you see? Different."

"Sure I see. But I'm mostly the same." He ran his free hand down his arm, the fine gold hairs there slicking flat, and she saw that under his tan his skin was burned. "My great Irish heritage. Mom keeps telling me I'll get skin cancer. She knew this dude once with no nose from skin cancer. That's her message for me this summer." He laced his fingers through hers, adjusting his grip. Their hands were exactly the same size; they'd measured once. We could be twins, she'd said. If you didn't have that curly dark hair, he'd said. Anyway, twin *hands,* they said at the same time, and their heads bumped when they laughed.

"You look good," she told him. "For a guy with a nose."

"So do you. Look good."

She pushed at her hair. "I feel gross. I took two showers but I still feel dirty. The air inside the plane had this recycled smell, and you knew everyone was breathing the same air. There was no air of your own."

He swung their hands between them, like a gate — open, closed, open.

"Do you want to come in?"

He studied the house again, as though peeling away the walls, looking inside the rooms. "They here?"

"Dad's asleep. Mom's upstairs reading or something."

"We could get some beers."

"Is anybody around?"

"Everybody's shipped off to college except me and Brian. We take turns guarding until the pool shuts down next weekend. Brian's totally wasted all the time. If he had to go in after anyone he'd drown with them."

She took his other hand, moved closer. There was a sheen of sweat on his upper lip. "How about you?"

"Like usual. Now and then."

"Your dad still giving you grass?"

He rubbed his lower lip, wiped the zinc oxide onto his jeans, rubbed again. After a moment, he said, "Yeah. Excellent grass."

"Terrific!"

"I don't know. I just don't think it's right and I've thought about it a lot lately. I don't think a father ought to give his kid grass. Parents should just stay parents, even if they piss you off and ride your ass about stupid stuff like getting sunburned. Dad gives me this 'ole buddy' grin and slips me a sandwich bag of his stuff."

She tried to get a clear focus on his frown in the fading light. "You used to be glad enough."

"I've done some thinking lately."

"You'd *buy* it, even if he didn't give it to you."

He looked down at his feet. "But it'd be *my* decision. You don't get it. I'm talking about values."

"Oh." She hadn't thought much about values. It hadn't occurred to her that Kit might. "Let's go get those beers."

She wondered what else he'd been thinking about since she saw him last. The night before he left they'd gone down to the beach on Lake Michigan, where they skipped stones on the calm lake. He'd leaned her against the guardrail there, his hands on her hair, lifting it and smoothing it on her shoulders, his lips near her own, his hands on her bare shoulders, then, the faintest weight of his chest against her sundress and breasts. "I really like you," he said. But he hadn't bent to her mouth and really kissed her, although she'd leaned against him as hard as she dared. He was shy. He was nineteen and had two older brothers, but he was shy. His oldest brother, who had gone into the liquor business with their dad, knocked up a girl he hardly knew and had to marry her when he was just Kit's age, Kit had told her once; it had taken him several tries to get that story out, his stuttering growing worse the more he tried. She hadn't asked him any more.

He had his car started by the time she'd climbed in her side. "So tell me all about your trip."

She sighed; she wasn't really interested in the trip. "We saw all this stuff Mom has been reading about for her entire life. Dad jogged in all the major cities. I ate a lot of chocolate. That's about it."

"Shit. Any parties?"

"How would I go to any parties?"

"I thought you might have met some guys or something." He turned toward town, gunning his car so that gravel scattered.

"When you travel with your folks you don't meet guys." She touched his leg, the soft denim. "Did you think about me?"

"How could I forget you? All those letters." He reached for her hand again, and pulled her across the plastic seat toward him. "Of course I thought about you." He had to work hard to get "thought" out, but she waited, she always waited, he'd told her to. "Like maybe you'd come back different."

"Different how?" She touched her hair. It was almost down to her collar; maybe he'd liked it shorter.

"I don't know. Things happen."

She leaned away from his shoulder to watch his profile—straight nose, hair he'd let grow covering his ears. The clean smell of him made her chest ache in a peculiar way. "What did you think about when you thought of me?"

"I just thought about you."

"How?"

"How guys think about girls, I guess."

"How do guys think about girls?"

He turned right along the railroad tracks toward the nearest spot they could buy beer. "You're teasing me." He had to work hard to say it, and he pinched her leg just above the knee.

The pinch hurt—a warning—stop it. He was right, she was teasing. She wanted attention. God, she was such a child. "Tell me what's been going on since you got back from your camp." It was the best she could do for an apology.

So he told her. He'd registered at Lake County College, which would be a waste of time, but his grades hadn't been good enough to get into the university. If he could get his grades up, he could transfer at the semester. He and Brian had found a bar up near Kenosha where they had live music on Saturday nights, blue grass. He'd take her there. Brian was going out to Colorado to live with his brother, who was logging. He'd miss old Brian. But he'd met a new guy, Phil Kien, who was one of the other counselors at camp. He and Phil were going to get an apartment together out in Liberty-ville where rents were cheaper. His mom didn't like the idea but he was sick of living at home with his mom and dad always yelling. He had to make the break sometime and this was it. He could afford it. He had a job loading UPS trucks at night after the pool job was over. Of course his dad always gave him money, just threw down some bucks on his dresser. He'd had to open a savings account because if it was lying around Brian took it. Anyway, he wanted to make it on his own without his dad's money. His dad had another new boat, inboard, twenty-two feet. He was always asking Kit to go fishing with him and his buddies, but who wanted to fish? That was about it.

"Who's this Phil guy?"

"He's from Northbrook. One of the senior counselors. He led our retreats and stuff like that. He's got good ideas."

"Like getting an apartment?" She watched the red and blue neon lights of the stores flash on his face. "You don't know how to cook."

"What's so hard about that? I figure you go to the store and you get some stuff and cook it."

"What kind of stuff?"

"Phil has it all worked out scientifically. You have to have protein — that's meat, eggs, cheese. Then vegetables like lettuce and carrots. Milk, of course. Cereal. Stuff to munch on, like cookies."

"That's the Nutrition Wheel, fourth grade! I can see those pictures of food groups in primary colors."

He laughed. "Shit, it'll be fine. Just because I don't know how to do something doesn't mean I can't learn."

The lights from the liquor store were green, wavering over the gravel parking lot like the shallows of the lake. Kit got a six-pack and they headed for the park up by the fort. The cops drove through every hour or so, but it was the best they could do this close to home. They didn't give you grief if you kept your booze in the car.

Kit popped a beer for her and one for himself and stashed the others under a towel on the back seat. The beer can was cold and she held it between her thighs, feeling the dampness soak her Levis. She listened to the racket from the cicadas and smelled the sweetly rank scent of goldenrod from the side ditch and oil from Kit's car. His shoulder was tense against hers and she leaned against him. "What else have you been doing?"

"I read some stuff." He wiped his mouth with the back of his hand, pushed around so his back was against the door and he could look at her. Her shoulder was chilled where his had been.

"Read what?"

"Dad's got all these books that came with the new house we

bought. A lot aren't real books, just cardboard to fill up the shelves. But there are some real ones, too. I read this stuff by Ernest Hemingway, *For Whom the Bell Tolls,* and *The Old Man and the Sea,* which is about this old man who goes fishing on the gulf."

"I thought you didn't like fishing." The beer filled her mouth with bitter coolness, traveled down through her chest where it warmed her belly.

"It's different in the book. The fish is like a symbol. And I've been reading statistics."

Jo took another long drink and groaned. She was terrible in math. "Why do you want to *read* it?"

"I'm planning ahead. I figure I'll get a start on it. Just once I'd like to get good grades. I mean really good grades. Phil says you have to think about the future, not just the present. Everything you do now has some bearing on the future. It's all connected."

So it was Phil who had brought "values" into Kit's life. She guessed she'd be hearing more about Phil. "That's a good plan," she said, thinking it would be nice to be excellent at something. Her mom had a Phi Beta Kappa key that she kept in with her earrings. She said good grades were a matter of discipline. Kit certainly had discipline when he needed it. When he'd gone out for soccer he'd practiced until he couldn't stand up. In track he'd never shorted the training miles; in wrestling he'd kept his weight down by locking himself in his room at mealtimes and chewing gum. She put her hand on his knee. "You'll get good grades if you decide to. You really will."

"You think so?"

"I know it. You'll be the star of Lake County College and I'll be the star of Woodcliff, handing in those little essays right on time, no excuses, footnotes and all. We'll be superstars on the academic scene."

Kit finished his beer and reached around the seat for another. He popped it and rested it against his forehead, then his temples, studying her around the edge of the sweating can. "Do you think this is going to be a horrible year? I mean, what do you really think?"

She thought it over. She'd applied to the interesting colleges too late and she was left going to a dinky girls' school. He was going to a county college with burn-outs and housewives. She'd be living at home, which was the same as being in high school. He'd have a crummy apartment that leaked when it rained. They'd both be thinking the whole time how to make things better the next year. Still, it wasn't her nature to be pessimistic. Who knows what will happen next? "I think it will be okay," she said, meaning it, and leaned to kiss his cheek. "Really okay. We have to start somewhere."

Kit set his beer on the dash and reached past her to the glove compartment, where he kept his grass. He took out a wooden box with a Boy Scout emblem carved on it, and quickly and expertly rolled a joint, lit it, passed it to her.

The smoke came into her lungs as smoothly as honey. "This is the new stuff your dad's getting?"

Kit took a hit. "What do you think?"

"Terrific." She took the J back from him.

"Take it easy. It's so good it'll knock you out."

"Good." The gold honey flowed through her chest, her arms, her legs. In the soft light from the distant street lamp, Kit's face had the same amber sheen as the polished wooden box he turned in his hands.

"I made this in wood-working, can you believe that? Sixth grade." He'd showed her once how he sorted his grass through the open-work sides of a silver tray his mother kept for calling cards. "Use what you have," he'd said. Now he handed her his industrial arts project, the box.

The smell of the dope it contained made her mouth pucker the way a green apple did. She let the box, with its pleasant patina, rest in her lap. She felt herself grinning. "Maybe it'll be a great year." She closed her eyes, leaned her head back against the crisp seatcover. Kit lifted the box from her legs, and she heard the snap of the glove compartment. The music of the night meadow was louder, as if the volume of the tree frogs and locusts had been turned up. A wind stirred in the pines. Kit's breath was on her cheek.

"I did miss you," he whispered. "I didn't want to say. I thought maybe you didn't miss me."

"I missed you," she whispered back without opening her eyes. "A lot. I thought about you. I thought about kissing you."

After a long moment in which, even through the sweet haze, she

imagined she'd pushed shy Kit too far, she felt his breath on her
mouth, and then, very softly, his lips. Neither of them moved. After
a moment she parted her lips to breathe and he parted his so that
their breath mingled. She timed herself so that she breathed in when
he breathed out. She was light-headed and floating. His mouth, or
maybe hers, was sweet like mint and tart like the smoke they shared.
She held very still, moving neither toward him nor away. His breath
filled her lungs and she swayed, underwater. After a long while he
moved back and they each took another hit on the joint, stubbing
it out to save it.

"Do that again?" she asked. He kissed her softly, as before, lips
parted. But this time instead of the breathing game she felt the tip
of his tongue. A slow caress, exploratory, first just inside her upper
lip where the most delicate membrane was, and then — how much
longer? — inside her lower lip. It was the most wonderful caress she'd
ever felt, and it moved through her body with the syrupy smoke.
"Let me," she said.

He curled his hands around the back of her neck and she licked
his lips slowly, as he had hers, then licked his teeth. After a while
he opened his mouth more and she did too, and there was a long
time in which, except for their tongues, they didn't move at all. The
night hum of the field flowed through the open windows of the car
like a warm current of water; they could breathe under this dark
water, it was a friendly element that bore them along gently.

Then abruptly he pushed away from her and dropped his hands
to her shoulders. She pressed her face against his throat, tasting salt.
Dazed.

"Jo, I've got to take it easy."

"Take it easy?"

"This is a really big test of my values."

"Values?" Had she heard him right?

"You know."

She shook her head, not understanding, wishing they'd just kiss
again. Even the soles of her feet ached with wanting to kiss. She
licked his damp throat experimentally, thinking on the next trade
she'd ask for that.

But he pulled away, took her hand in his, and held their clasped hands between them. He could push her away, but he couldn't make her open her eyes; she wanted to let the water pull them under again.

"Are you listening?"

"I guess," she said.

"I've been trying to think things through."

"Yes." She drew out the sound. Yes was part of the song from the fields around them.

"I mean, I've got to get some stuff right for a change. Everything in my life is second-rate. That's the truth. Second-rate family, no matter how much dough is around, second-rate crummy jobs, a second-rate crummy little college out in the sticks. I figure I've got to do better. It's the only life I've got, and I don't want all this crummy getting-by, like my folks have."

She kept her eyes closed tightly. Why was his voice so stern? "I'm second-rate for you?"

"No, not you! I mean all the rest of it."

She rubbed her face against his shoulder, his chest hot through his soft cotton shirt. "Why are you telling me now?"

"I have to."

"You could tell me later."

"*Now.* Like I have to take charge of who I am, what I do. Like with sex."

He paused and she snuggled closer, their clasped hands against her breasts. "Sex," she repeated.

"You asked me what guys think about when they think about girls. They think about getting a piece. That's it. That's *all.* I don't want to be like that. Most guys want to get high and get laid, and they don't even care if they know the name of the girl they're screwing, that's the truth. Like my own brother Danny, who'd only been out with Carol once and didn't even *like* her and got her pregnant. And her folks are Catholic and my brother's supposed to be and she said no abortion, it's a sin. So now they're married."

She nodded against his chest.

"I want to get love right, like in the Hemingway book. Not just screwing, but love. See?"

She nodded again, her forehead bumping his chin. "I don't have to get pregnant."

"But like my *value* is love. That comes first."

She opened her eyes and saw his face as a dark shape exactly in front of her own. She couldn't make out his expression, but his skin seemed to radiate a shimmering heat. "Let's kiss some more, Kit."

"It's awful tough on me," he said, as though confessing to an unusual weakness. "And I found Jesus this summer," he added.

"Jesus?" She pulled back to get a better look at him.

"I've been a Catholic all my life, but I'd never found Jesus."

"Is there a difference?" What did Jesus have to do with kissing?

"It's like I've taken Him for my personal savior and all."

That was something she'd never figured on. "Sin and all that?"

He settled back against the door again, apparently eager for a discussion. "Sin sounds so heavy. Negative. Most Catholics are real negative. But some are real positive, those who've found Jesus. It's a whole different point of view. Like my mom talks about the stuff you shouldn't do — don't do this, don't do that — and of course Dad does what he wants to anyway. When you truly find Jesus you think of the things you *should* do. It's easy when you believe. It's like falling in love, I guess, everything is just so clear and simple. There's a lot I don't believe in, like the birth control thing, but I feel really good about Jesus. He's helped me work out my values and go for long-term goals. Like love."

She took a deep breath and tried to clear her head. "How does Jesus feel about kissing?"

He answered carefully, as though he'd thought it out and gone over it time and again, in preparation for her question. "Kissing is a sign of love and affection. There's not a thing wrong with it. It's a symbol. That's no problem. The problem for me is that I'm afraid I can't stop with just kissing. And I don't want to go farther."

She narrowed her eyes, trying to see his expression in the swaying light. His lips were set. He'd made a decision.

First she was angry, maybe even bitter; didn't what *she* wanted matter? Then suddenly she felt like laughing out loud at her discovery, and had to bite her lips to keep from giggling. It was just her luck; he was saving himself for love. She smiled at him in the dark, feeling like his mom for a moment, or like his older sister, anyway, amused but tender. He was also telling her that he didn't love her. Maybe he would love her, but right now he didn't. She gave him credit for telling the truth. She didn't love him either, although she certainly wanted to kiss him some more. She liked him. He was a good guy. But she didn't know what she was going to do about Kit-and-Jesus.

She tried to think what to say and came up with, "Thanks for telling me." It sounded formal to her, but he hugged her, his hot face against her hair.

"You don't think I'm crazy, do you? I'm not in a cult or anything. I'm just really a believer."

"I think you're okay. I mean it. How about Phil? Is he a believer, too?"

"We plan to spend weekends working on retreats for Catholic kids, helping them to understand." He touched her cheek, gently. "Jo, do *you* understand? Is there anything else I can tell you?"

"I'll think about what you've said." She looked back over the seat, pretending to check for cops. She was afraid again that she would laugh, though nothing at all that Kit said was really funny.

He pulled her close again, bumping her hip against the steering wheel. "You smell so good, Jo. You smell like those little white flowers that bloom in April and no one's supposed to pick them."

She realized that it had been several minutes since he'd stuttered. He must be at peace with himself, or maybe it was the grass. "Can we have another hit of that excellent J? Then I've got to go home. I've got such a jet-lag headache I feel silly." That was in case she did laugh, in spite of her efforts. She pretended to yawn to hide her smile.

They smoked a little more, and then he drove her home, slowly, his arm around her shouders, smiling at her from time to time.

"Mellow?" she asked.

"I just never thought you'd understand."

She drank her second beer while he drove. She felt sad, now, as though the possibility for loving him had closed up just as it had begun to open. She wanted more kissing like that. She wanted her whole body kissed like that. Instead, it looked to her like she and Kit were going to be buddies. She sighed.

"Sleepy?" He squeezed her shoulder.

"Very." The truth was that she was lonely.

At her house he walked her to the porch, kissed her quickly on the cheek. "I'll call you, okay?"

When she opened the door her golden retriever came running, belly low to the floor with pleasure. Under her hands the dog turned in circles, tail slapping Jo's arms and legs. She crouched to press her face into the soft, musty coat. She started to laugh, although when she put her hand to her face she found that she was crying, too, dog hair stuck to her cheeks. She kept her arms tightly around her dog, imagining Kit's face close to hers in the dark, his chin set with his new moral certitude. Then she imagined how a man might kiss a woman he loved.

"Oh, Kit!" she said against the dog's soft ear. "You bastard!"

Some of the Things I Did Not Do

Before my mother poured gasoline over herself and burned herself to death in the hog barn, she wrote me a letter. She left it on the kitchen counter under an empty macaroni-and-cheese box. My neighbor, Ray Quinn, one of the volunteer firemen, found the letter and gave it to me. It was about all the guys could do when they got there, her place so far out from town and all of them picking corn this time of year. The blue envelope was sealed. "Sheriff will probably want to see this, Nick," Ray told me as he handed it over. "For evidence of mental illness." As if there could be any question about the mental health of a woman who torches herself in a hog barn.

I took the letter out to my pickup. I had a pint of Jack Daniels in my glove compartment, and I wanted some — wanted a lot — but made myself drink a little, slow, from one of Mom's jelly glasses. She'd written my full name on the envelope — Nicholas John Heilman — and the letter was written on fancy notepaper I didn't even know she had, a border like a blossoming branch along the top of the single page.

> Nick dear,
>
> I'm bad and getting worse and the angels won't come.
> I thought I saw some today, but no, just crows on
> the barn roof. I'm so tired, honey. If the angels
> aren't going to come I'm calling it quits anyway.
> Sometimes Our Lord just wants too much. More than's
> good for Him, if you know what I mean.
>
> Your Momma

I made sure I didn't look toward the caved-in ruin of the hog barn where they were bagging what was left of her. I drank some more. Then I walked over to Ray and the others who were winding up the hoses, and said thanks for stopping by, as though they'd been paying a Sunday visit for beers and tv football.

"Don't think nothing of it," Ray said. He didn't look at me. "Lucky the fire didn't hurt the livestock."

That reminded me and I went to feed the hogs before I drove into town to see the sheriff.

He read Mom's letter. "Nick, what's this stuff about angels?" He scratched the loose skin under his jaw. Under his office lights his face looked wavery, like the surface of moving water. I held onto his desk.

"She was crazy, Pete, you know that. She thought angels were going to fly in to carry her away."

"I see you don't want to talk about it."

"I don't mind. Facts are facts."

"We won't talk about it, then." I saw he'd written "suicide" on a legal-looking form that lay in front of him on the scarred desk top. "Why the hell don't you go on home and get some rest. You still in that trailer out on Route K?"

"Couple of miles past her place."

"I'll stop by tomorrow and we'll make plans for her funeral."

"And bury *what?*"

"Nick, have another drink. Get some rest."

"Burn her house down, too!" I told him, and wished I hadn't when he teared up.

"There's procedures." He wiped his nose on his greasy sleeve.

"Screw procedures."

"In the morning you'll feel better. You need help with her farm?"

"I look after it. Who do you think's been looking after it? Not her. Praying took up all her time." Which wasn't fair to say, because Mom and I had planned that out: she paid me for the work I did on her place, and she paid Uncle Leon for his part, too—she had some money from Dad's GI insurance. I got out of Pete's office fast before I could say anything else or he could say how after all maybe it was better this way.

An October evening, warm and hazy, the sun a red blur at the horizon. Shadows filled the side ditches and the drone of grasshoppers hummed in the hedgerows as loud as my truck engine. In the hollows bugs smashed up on my windshield and I smelled the sour smoke from fields being burned off. That made me think about Mom, but I was also checking to see who'd got their crops in; growing up with Mom had taught me how to slice up my thoughts into compartments. I had to keep two things in mind at once — her truth, and how things really were. For example, sometimes Mom thought I was the devil come to tempt her. There I was, a skinny kid with string-bean arms and straw-yellow hair that needed cutting, and she'd be hiding from me in the broom closet. Or, because I usually wore Dad's army fatigue jacket and hat, sometimes she thought I was him, come back from Korea after all. What a mess. That part sapped my spirits, no doubt about it. Every year or so, when she'd go off like that, I'd walk across the field to Uncle Leon's and he'd come drive her to Mendota and get her committed. Psychotic break. Paranoid schizophrenic. Big words. They'd drug her up and in a few weeks she'd be out to pick me up from Uncle Leon's like claiming me from Lost and Found. She'd apologize and apologize, as though she'd done something wrong, guilty because she'd got sick. Then she'd start in praying again. The angels were gonna make it all better, sure they were.

I was gunning down the road, thinking how I'd head for the south now, though I knew I wouldn't, when I saw a station wagon, hood up, emergency light flashing. Even before I got close I saw whose it was, and I got a rush like another swig of whiskey, though I knew the last thing I needed right then was to be trying to help a woman who didn't want one single thing I had to give her. I pulled up behind the car and slammed out of my truck. I saw her watching me in her rearview mirror.

"You again?" she said. Sweet Sue.

She sat there looking disgusted behind the steering wheel of her Datsun, but pretty as always, her dark hair loose on the shoulders of her sweater that had something glittery woven in with the wool. One of her little girls knelt beside her in the front seat and peered up at me with eyes as big and unblinking as a raccoon's.

"Looks like you got trouble, Susy."

"*Susan*. Trouble *owns* me, or have you forgotten."

"You shouldn't have got one of these toys. Buy American."

"For god's sake will you just drive on! I don't need you telling me *should*." She shook her fist at me, meaning it. She'd hit me once, in my ribs, just like she was a boxer. Sharp fist, and it hurt like hell. She slugged me because she wanted to get it straight with me, she said. Men had always told her what to do and how to be and she couldn't live like that any more. I said I could understand how that would make her angry, but what did that have to do with us? So she socked me again. She hit me because I wanted to get married and she didn't — figure that one out.

I leaned on her open hood and gave that little motor the once over. Funny how that good oil smell will straighten out your head. Battery was all right, sparks plugged in. "Just quit on you?"

"I pulled over because Donna said she was going to throw up. Then it wouldn't start again."

"Got a pencil?"

"I've got four pencils and thirty exams to grade and Donna and Dianne haven't even had supper and it's almost eight o'clock. Why the hell a pencil?" She handed me a yellow one out of her canvas bag.

I slid the pencil into the valve and motioned for her to start her up again. She shoved hard on the key and the gas, and it flared right up with that whine those cars have.

Another blonde head appeared from the back seat; either Donna or Dianne had been napping back there — twins. I never did learn to tell them apart. "Mommy, where *are* we?"

"Almost home, thanks to my hero here." She gave me one of her turned-down smiles and shrugged.

I closed the hood and leaned down to her window. "So, here's the plan. You drive on home and I'll follow you to make sure you get there. You got only a few miles to go."

"It's out of your way."

"I don't mind."

"*I* mind."

"What have I got to lose?"

"What a life," she sighed.

By which I knew she meant to thank me. She didn't like to say thank you, she often told me. People should just do what they wanted to, not trying to please. I liked pleasing her—nothing I could do about that—my problem, not hers, as she pointed out.

"So how you been doing?" I asked her, to keep her a moment longer. The smell of her talc hurt my chest.

"Like always."

"Always used to be pretty busy."

"What can you do? At least I've got my job. They've been laying off teachers all over the county. Donna had chicken pox and couldn't go to the regular sitter; that's been the worst."

So that must be Donna, then, with her head buried in Susan's lap, pulling her momma's plaid skirt into a cuddling blanket and sucking her thumb.

"Someone told me there was a fire over near your mom's, Nick. Maybe the silo."

"The hog barn."

"Too bad."

"Mom was in it."

"Nick!"

"She set the fire. Set fire to herself, actually." When I saw Susan's face crumple I wished I'd thought of another way to say it.

"Oh, god!" When she shook her head her tears webbed out onto her temples.

"It's okay."

"How can it be *okay?*"

"I mean, one way's as good as another."

"I'm thinking of her whole life, Nick!"

"I am too."

"But she *knew* she was going to do that!"

"Sometimes she didn't."

"But when she *did* know! Imagine living like that, knowing you were going to go crazy again, go wandering around in the fields to look for help."

"Looking for angels."

Susan cried harder. She used to cry after we'd made love, her face on my chest, her hands digging into my shoulders. Once I understood why I didn't mind; everything just let go all at once, she said, good feelings and then old pain come again. I liked holding her then, my chest and her face all wet and the smell of loving still on us.

"She wrote me that she guessed the angels weren't coming after all."

"Shut up, Nick!" As though Mom belonged to her, not me.

I swatted the side of her car with my open palm. "She was crazy and she wanted to die."

"And you're not sorry?"

"I'm damn sorry for all of us, her no more than you or me or your little girls."

She stopped crying then, pushed back her hair, and rubbed her nose. "You're a bitter man, Nick."

"Maybe."

"But I don't believe you."

"You never did."

"I don't believe you're not hurting inside."

"I'm not hurting inside."

"I don't believe you aren't smothering down your grief."

"Well, I'm not. I'm glad it's over, if you want to know."

"Mommy!" The girl, Dianne I guess, crawled over from the back seat into the front, her overalls soaked between her legs. She lay down by her sister. The twins slept together in one bed, back to belly. The way Susan and I had slept. "Go home, Mommy!" Both kids whimpered a lot.

"Nick, listen, no matter what I'm saying right now, I'm really sorry. When you remember seeing me tonight, remember that I'm really, really sorry." She put her warm hand on my wrist and I realized the night had come on cooler than I'd thought.

"Susan, I do not need the sorrow of a good woman."

Violently, she rolled her window part way up, and I put my hand on the glass so she wouldn't roll it higher, though I knew my hand wouldn't stop her if she was angry enough. She'd drive off with me dragging along beside her in the dust, if she got that into her head. "Susan—I need you, but not your pity."

"I'm more or less sick of hearing how you don't need pity. So what, you lost your foot," she sing-songed. "So what, your mom is dead.

You're doing fine, right? Mister superman!" Her hiss carried her breath to me, mints and cigarettes.

I wanted both to kiss her and to slap her — at the same time. We were right back where we'd left off, just when it came to me how much I'd been hoping she'd say, Come have supper, stay with me, just to sleep, that's all. But no, we messed it up, as usual.

"The way I see it is you got to get home and fix your kids some chow. Personally, I'm heading back to my place, and if I know you're home safe I'll rest easier as I eat my tv dinner. It's over for Mom, and she'd say that's a blessing. That's how it is for me, okay?"

"Okay," she said in that small voice she used when she felt misunderstood.

Before she could say anything else I headed back to my truck, making sure I wasn't limping more than usual since she'd brought it up again about my foot. Once she tried to touch my stump. "You've got to learn to love this," she said. I knocked her off the bed. Poor Susan, she had her work cut out for her, with me yelling at her in my sleep, "They're coming! Coming!" I couldn't hear or see them but I knew the gooks were right there in the trees. At least when the mine went off under me there was the explosion. The roar was reassuring in a way; something horrible had happened and the noise confirmed it.

She threw gravel pulling back onto the asphalt. I caught up to her easy, but I stayed back, giving her lots of room. "Breathing space," she'd tell me. And once, "You take up too much room in here, Nick." That was the night I got to her house before she did and fixed us all a tuna and noodle casserole, the recipe right on the back of the noodle package, just add a can of tuna, one of soup, and chips on top. Tasted all right. She took it as an insult. "You're taking over," she yelled even before she'd got her jacket off.

While I served the little girls pulled their stools up to the counter.

"You can't *do* this."

"I got here first, and I was hungry. I figured you and the kids would be, too."

"We've got left-over meatloaf."

"Don't you liberated chicks want men who cook?"

She wouldn't eat the dinner I made. She munched cold meatloaf on toast and the kids and I finished up the whole casserole. When they were in bed Susan told me, "I won't have you treating me like you treat your mom."

"Like my *mom!*" That one really pole-axed me.

"You cook for her. You take stuff to her place because she's helpless. You told me you never knew if there'd be meals or not when you were growing up. Well, I'm not like her."

"You just said a mouthful. You're nothing on this planet like my mom, and that's a fact."

The funny thing was, after all, she did seem a little bit like my mom. I don't mean in the crazy ways. But sometimes they smiled in the same way—that kind of dazed, blurry smile a woman has when she forgets to worry.

Once I saw Mom smiling at the tomatoes I'd planted for 4-H. She was squatting down between the plants, her skirt hem in the dust, her straw hat shading her face. My vines were just loaded down with fruit, red and green and yellow tomatoes coming along.

"See here, Nicky, your beauties!" They filled her hands.

She was pretty when she smiled. Uncle Leon told me that made it easier for her; they'd take better care of her in the hospital because she was a looker. At least when she was younger. When she got older she kept that softness, like I was older than she was; because she didn't worry about the same things as the rest of us. She was like a kid, like Donna or Dianne. That wasn't her fault, but it was up to me to do the laundry, cook supper, slop the hogs, and go to my work. She sat on the porch swing and rocked, watched the sky, braided her brown hair and then unbraided it again. I did love her, but that's no kind of a mother to have.

Of course she didn't choose to be like that. When she was "clear," as she called her sane days, she wrote on the lined sheets of my notebook paper, regular essays on the topic of why folks should have the right to choose whether they're going to live or die. She had a real fine cursive, and organized opening paragraphs, topic sentences, logical conclusions. Because she hadn't graduated from high school, she made me read them all to correct her spelling and such, though I never could see she made any errors. Then she'd copy them over, tear the sheets out of my spiral notebook, and trim the raggy edges with kitchen shears before sending the essays off to our congressmen and state representatives. Of course she didn't get much response, just a lot of xeroxed flyers. What could anyone say—sure, go on and pull the plug, lady?

"It is a death in life to live like this," she wrote. "When things are clear for me, I'm expecting all the time that I will go under again. It is a living hell for me and my son. I should be allowed the right, not the privilege, of removing myself from this torment." She'd follow my reading along, her lips forming the words. At such times my heart would slam down, like a window falling closed suddenly in a storm: there's the howl of the rain and then the crash and then silence.

But when she licked a stamp and addressed the envelopes, Mom had that pleased, little kid smile—like now she'd done something to fix our life. As if it could be fixed. Her smile would make me feel safe for a moment, even though I knew better.

The first time I saw that same smile on Susan's face, we were at my place and we'd had some beers, there were country tunes on the radio, and I was showing her I could still dance. We were bumping up against the counters and the stove, me trying to dip her and her trying to boogie. Then I lifted her up with my arms around her waist and I guess she forgot for a while how hard it was to manage and no support money coming in from the kids' dad and nothing ahead but more of the same. Because she gave me this smile like nothing existed except just that moment, the two of us roughhousing around, not wanting especially even to make love, just hanging onto each other and laughing. It was like suddenly I could breathe deep down in my whole body where I hadn't had any air for maybe my whole life.

There were a few of those good times, not many. I was traveling one way, she was going another, as she said. I wanted to settle down and have kids, the whole works. She said she'd been there and done that and I could save myself a whole lot of time and trouble, not to mention bucks, if I'd take her word that marriage was a bummer. And why would she want to marry a crippled farmer who yelled in his sleep—though she didn't say that.

When Susan pulled into the drive of the little place she was renting, she beeped me a so-long, shave-and-a-haircut. I pulled off the road while I made sure she got inside. I had helped her out, after all. Towards the last, when she said she couldn't see us going on like that, I'd said, "Maybe we could just be friends."

"Being friends is the hardest thing of all, Nick. Much harder than being married. There aren't any maps for being friends." As though she'd thought that one through, along with everything else.

"I could help you out, you could help me."

"But there *is* no way to help you. And I'm managing on my own."

"You are such a stubborn chick!"

"We'll see," was all she'd say.

I hadn't had much chance to follow up on helping her out, except to put up a railing around her porch so the kids wouldn't tumble off, and to mow her lawn. After the last time I mowed, I brought out my old softball and she played catch with me in the sideyard. She had good moves. "Put more arc on it!" she yelled, like it was a slow-pitch game for the championship. I couldn't run, but she threw them right at me, her tongue pressed against her upper lip and her bare legs covered with grass clippings.

When I saw lights go on inside her house I pulled away, thinking how when I raked her leaves maybe I'd take over my old football. I could throw, and she could run out for passes.

That idea nerved me up, and I decided to stop by Mom's before I went home. Get it over. But as soon as I set foot inside her kitchen I knew I shouldn't have come. She'd made everything *ready*. It was cleaned up careful for a woman who didn't take any interest in housekeeping. She'd put her coats on hangers instead of just the pegs, her yellow macintosh and the tweed she wore to church. An empty grocery bag for trash sat by the stove, the dustpan and broom there, too. The counter tops were all clean, her rinsed dishes in the drainer, only the macaroni dish left soaking in the sink. Her old sheepskin slippers were just inside the door where I stood; she must have slipped on her boots before she went out to the hog barn.

The mercury vapor lights from the drive laid vine shadows on the table before I turned on the reading lamp, then the pink roses on the oilcloth jumped at me. The kitchen smelled of bacon, and I caught myself thinking that was a good sign; when I was a kid and woke smelling breakfast cooking I'd know things were okay. You learn to pay attention to things like that. So the smoke-cured smell would have been a good piece of news. Except that it wasn't.

Tacked up on the wall by the table were postcards I'd sent her over the years, a few from 4-H camp, one from a class trip to Washington, a couple of flimsy cards with pictures of temples I'd sent from Nam. She had the message sides turned to the wall. Below the cards were two newspaper clippings, one about my hog winning a blue at the state fair, and another about my Purple Heart. Both of them were about an inch and a half long, like they weighed about the same in the editor's mind. Beside the clippings was a snapshot Uncle Leon took of me and Mom when I graduated from high school. My hair was getting long, and I was wearing my country-hippie work shirt. She was in her good blue suit, her hair soft along her cheeks, shading her eyes with her hand because she thought her straw hat wasn't dressy enough. Her jacket was snug over her bosom. That meant she must have just got out of the hospital, where she always put on weight. So loud, she told me, everyone on the ward screaming and crying in spite of the drugs. "They feed us all the time to keep us quiet." Which was just as well, because at home she forgot about meals. I'd bring her what I'd fixed for my dinner, or set something out on her counter so she couldn't overlook it — canned chili, soup, macaroni and cheese.

In the snapshot she clutched the big purse Uncle Leon gave her, large enough to hold her toilet articles, brush and comb, billfold, her drawing pad and crayons, even her slippers. In the hospital she slept with her purse for a pillow. If you laid something down it was stolen. Her big purse wasn't on the table where she always kept it when she was home.

Instead, there was a stack of those notebooks, the ones she wrote her essays in, like she'd left them there for me to correct one more time. Under them were the folders in which she kept the replies she'd got back in the mail. I got her empty trash bag and pushed it all in, thinking to take it on my next trip to the dump. On the bottom of the stack I found a single sheet of manila paper. I guessed she'd run out of notebook pages and overflowed onto the drawing paper

they gave her in occupational therapy. I was about to crumple that
sheet, too, when I saw it was a list. Neat numbers down the left-
hand side, one through twenty. Title at the top:

> *Some of the Things I Did Not Do*
> 1) struck him, not even by accident.
> 2) never without a roof over our heads.
> 3) kept the cats out of the house because of his allergies.
> 4) never put him down like I've heard some do their boys,
>   but he aims to please, so this may not count.

There were sixteen more numbers on the page, but no more entries.
I wondered if she'd run out of things to write, or if she'd just decided
to get on with it, wrote me her good-bye letter, and, as she said,
called it quits.

The way she'd reckoned herself up laid me so low I had to sit down
at the table. Lined up on the oilcloth were a mason jar of brown
figs a neighbor must have brought her, butter spoon-packed into
a coffee cup, and the donkey planter I made in fifth grade art.
Although the planter held pennies and nickels now, when I brought
it home that Christmas it held a cactus: our theme was Mexico, Land
of the Sun. I dumped it into the trash bag, too, leaving the change
on the table for Goodwill, or whoever we could get to take her things
away. I ripped down the cards and clippings without bothering to
untack them, and tossed them in. I put the snapshot in my wallet.
Before I crumpled up her list, I took her pencil stub and printed

> 5) never lied. Not ever, though I wished you had. Maybe
>   that counts.

Then I smashed the paper into a ball and stuffed it in with the rest.

The moon was coming up, that fat, orange one, harvest moon,
though I knew it was only dust in the air that made it look so swollen
and ripe. I still had an inch of whiskey in my pint, and I let it run
hot down my throat. Then I eased off the parking brake, put the
truck into first, and let her just roll down the drive into the valley.
Coasting that way was floating on a dark river, the night chill pouring
into my open window like well water gushing cold. I was wondering
where was my bike pump—I wanted to fill the football—when wings
rushed up right by my head. I ducked, couldn't help it, even though

I knew all I'd done was to flush a pheasant from the unpicked corn-field. He came up clucking loud, his tail spread wide and silvery—no angel, though. Flapping heavily, he barely cleared the top of my truck. I braked to a stop to wait for the female. Wind rustled the dry stalks. There was a minute where I heard only my heart beating. Then, yes, there she came, the hen clattering up, smaller than the male but climbing higher, casting her shadow like a handprint across the moon as she passed over me to dive down after her mate into the rows of corn.

ILLINOIS SHORT FICTION

Crossings by Stephen Minot
A Season for Unnatural Causes by Philip F. O'Connor
Curving Road by John Stewart
Such Waltzing Was Not Easy by Gordon Weaver

Rolling All the Time by James Ballard
Love in the Winter by Daniel Curley
To Byzantium by Andrew Fetler
Small Moments by Nancy Huddleston Packer

One More River by Lester Goldberg
The Tennis Player by Kent Nelson
A Horse of Another Color by Carolyn Osborn
The Pleasures of Manhood by Robley Wilson, Jr.

The New World by Russell Banks
The Actes and Monuments by John William Corrington
Virginia Reels by William Hoffman
Up Where I Used to Live by Max Schott

The Return of Service by Jonathan Baumbach
On the Edge of the Desert by Gladys Swan
Surviving Adverse Seasons by Barry Targan
The Gasoline Wars by Jean Thompson

Desirable Aliens by John Bovey
Naming Things by H. E. Francis
Transports and Disgraces by Robert Henson
The Calling by Mary Gray Hughes

Into the Wind by Robert Henderson
Breaking and Entering by Peter Makuck
The Four Corners of the House by Abraham Rothberg
Ladies Who Knit for a Living by Anthony E. Stockanes